The
Chamber
of
Truth

John M. Burchfield

The Chamber of Truth

of

Truth

QUEST FOR THE JEWEL

John M. Burchfield

Manufactured in the United States of America

For information, please contact:

The P3 Press
16200 North Dallas Parkway, Suite 170
Dallas, Texas 75248
www.theP3press.com
972-381-0009

A New Era in Publishing™

ISBN-13: 978-1-933651-81-1
ISBN-10: 1-933651-81-4
LCCN: 2010910399
1 2 3 4 5 6 7 8 9 10

Author Contact info:
TheChamberofTruth@charter.net
www.JohnBurchfieldBooks.com

For Debby,
The finest woman
I have ever known.

For my son Aaron,
and my daughter Rebecca,
I will always love you!

Acknowledgments

Where does inspiration come from? In writing this story the inspiration was found among friends, family, and former colleagues. I thank them all. Not just for the good times, but also for those times that were not so good. Life experiences are what make each of us who we are, and I wouldn't change a thing. Yes, I've made plenty of mistakes and I have some regrets. But life experiences help us to understand who we are and what makes us tick.

I dedicate this story to the memory of my friend Leigh. She fought a battle of insurmountable odds, and she never lost her faith. She leaves a legacy rich in a spirit of determination and strong will, and she will live on forever in the hearts of her children and in our memories.

I could not have written this book without the love and support of my wife Debby. She is not only the finest woman I have ever known, she is without a doubt the finest person I have ever known. She is truly an angel here on earth. I thank the good Lord each day for allowing her to be such a wonderful part of my life. What a magnificent place this would be if everyone could find such a person to love and that is able to love with all of their heart, all of their mind, and all of their soul, as Debby so selflessly does each and every day.

Well, I hope you like the story. Happy reading!

Prologue

Tuesday afternoon. There was nothing particularly significant about the day aside from the frigid temperature. This was the fifth day in a row with temperatures hovering close to zero. There had not been a January this cold in the Holy City in fifteen years. As the temperature continued to drop, a light dusting of snow blanketed the region, and in the city, people were scurrying around as the day came to an end. Below the city, however, things were just beginning to heat up.

Deep within the bowels of the earth, a cavern was set so deep that neither sun nor moon shattered its darkness. In a small chamber located within this deep chasm, a single lit candle rested on the ground. The chamber was one of many that had been carved into the earth centuries ago. Every so often, the candle's flickering light revealed a shadowy image near the center of the chamber—that of a young man kneeling. But the young man was not praying. He was being held captive and forced to kneel, like a beggar, in the cold of the earth. The young man had been taken prisoner and was awaiting his execution. The entryway into the chamber was narrow, the air stale, and the floor made of hardened clay. Slowly the assassin circled his prisoner. Three times the assassin had made his demands. Three times the prisoner had provided an explanation. And, three times the young man was warned that his answer was unsatisfactory.

Finally, the assassin leaned in close, his foul breath creating a wreath around his prisoner's lowered head, and slowly he raised his dagger.

"Do you have any last words?" The prisoner did not respond. Death poised itself on the edge of silence. The prisoner was about to break when something caught his eye. He had been watching their shadows, cast by the candle's flickering flame, dancing back and forth across the cavern wall. But just for a moment, he thought he saw another image—one of a figure slipping through the small entryway into the chamber. Were his eyes playing tricks on him? No, the assassin had noticed it too. There was a slight change in the air, bringing with it a new, fresh odor. The assassin tilted his head and sniffed the air. He sniffed again; the air was sweet and clean. It was an aroma that the assassin had smelled before—*but where?* Distracted, he lowered his dagger and turned toward the entrance.

In contrast, the prisoner had instantly recognized the scent that filled the dank cave. He took a deep lungful. Lilacs. It smelled good. So good, in fact, that he let out a huge sigh, and he couldn't stop a smile from spreading across his face. Seeing his captive's growing laxity, the assassin quickly turned back and tried to regain his focus. With a renewed sense of urgency he was determined to dispatch his rival once and for all. Quickly he raised the dagger once again. As he lifted his arms over his head, he felt something press against his neck.

"Careful knight, that's a blade at your throat." The assassin's eyes darted to the left. The limited light prevented the assassin from seeing the face of the person who had so fully gained the advantage. From out of the darkness, a disembodied hand forced him to relinquish his dagger, slowly pulling it from the assassin's grip.

"Joseph. It's time to go," echoed a voice from the shadows. Slowly, the prisoner stood free from his captor and turned to face his would-be murderer.

"Sir Dark Knight. As my executioner you asked me if I had any last words. Well, I do. And here they are: 'Act as if ye have faith and faith shall be given, and ye shall be free.'"

"Again with the quoting! What is that supposed to mean?" spat the Dark Knight.

Joseph grinned, "Faith, my dear sir, is my freedom, and she is standing right behind you. M'lady, let's get out of here!" With that, Joseph turned and rushed through the doorway. He was closely followed by Rachel, his trusty sidekick and savior.

The Dark Knight was shouting behind them, "I will find you! I always do!" Joseph and Rachel said nothing— they were too busy running. Once again, they had managed to fend off the evil forces of the Dark Knight. Once again, Rachel had managed to get the upper hand. Running along the corridor, Joseph fumbled in the darkness for his flashlight. When he managed to get the light out of his pocket and switched on, he realized that they were in unfamiliar territory. A division in the passageway loomed ahead. Now they had to decide which way to go. One passageway appeared to slope up while the other continued downward. Without hesitation they took the passageway that sloped down. They ran until Joseph couldn't run anymore. He stopped, leaned over, and put his hands on his knees to catch his breath. He was exhausted. "Is he still behind us?" he huffed. There was no answer. He waited a few seconds and then asked, "Do you see him anywhere?" Still no response. Looking around, he found he was alone.

Slowly, he straightened up and took several more deep breaths. Retracing his steps, he turned and walked back up the corridor and stopped. Switching off his flashlight, he listened to the deathly quiet of the caves. He listened for what felt like hours, but it was only a few minutes. The only sounds he could hear were those of his own breathing. Switching his light back on he looked back up the corridor. He could see a faint shadow moving at the other end. Quickly he cut his light off and moved up against the wall, waiting and listening. Carefully, he inched his way back down the corridor. He switched the flashlight back on and scanned the walls. There were several small openings. Finally, in desperation, he whispered her name. "Rachel?" Immediately there was a response.

"I'm over here. Shine your light over here," she hissed.

"Where? Where are you?"

"Just follow my voice. I'm right over here."

"I can't follow your voice," said Joseph, exasperated. "You know how these walls make sounds echo. I could be standing right next to you and not even know it. Strike a match and let me see if I can find the flame."

Rachel took a small box of matches from her pocket and retrieved a match. With one flick of her wrist, the match was lit, and Joseph could see a soft orange light flickering not twenty feet away from within a recess in the cavern wall. With a hand against the wall to guide him, he moved toward her and found himself in a small cavern. As he entered, Joseph glanced cautiously around, "Rachel, what are you doing? We better go back. This place is a hive. There are chambers everywhere; we'll get lost."

"Relax, I thought I saw something in this one," she said. She was holding the match high above her head and looking at the ground.

"What do you mean you think there's something in this one?"

Rachel pointed toward the back of the small room, "Joseph, look!"

As Joseph turned he saw an eerie-looking figure perched in the corner, sitting, hunched over something on the cavern floor. Joseph quickly stepped in front of Rachel as if to shield her from any harm. Rachel, identifying the gesture, pushed past him, "Uh, thanks, but I think I'm OK. I just wanted to say that it looks like the old skeleton guy is guarding some kind of trunk."

Joseph shined his light toward the back of the room. "Wow, it looks like a treasure chest." He walked over to the trunk and dropped to his knees.

"He's missing a tooth," said Joseph, as he shined his light in the skeleton's mouth. "I wonder who he was. It looks like he was trying to protect the trunk, doesn't it?"

Pointing toward the skeleton, Rachel asked, "What's that around his neck?" Joseph leaned forward and took hold of a chain that was hung around the corpse's neck.

"It looks like some sort of medal with a jewel of some kind," said Joseph. Just then there was a noise behind them. Rachel jumped and turned around. Joseph stood and shined his light on the intruder.

"Ah hah! Your secret chamber has been discovered. Up with your hands!" demanded the intruder.

Rachel recognized the voice right away. "Saul! What are you doing?"

"I found you. I told you that I would," replied Saul shrugging.

Joseph stepped forward, gesturing behind him. "Saul, look what we have found. . . ."

"What? I'm no longer the Dark Knight?" asked Saul.

Joseph turned and moved his light toward the skeleton and the trunk. "Come on, no more games—this is serious."

"Okay, whatever you say. Well, well—what do we have here?" he drawled, dropping down beside Joseph.

"We don't know," said Rachel. "But it looks like he's been here for a long time. We think he was guarding this old trunk."

"What do you think is in it?" asked Joseph.

"There's only one way to find out," said Rachel. "Let's open it."

Joseph knelt back down in front of the chest and tucked the flashlight under his arm. He took a hold of the skeleton's bony hands and gently slid them off the trunk, leaning the skeleton's remains against the wall. Taking hold of the trunk's lid, he slowly began to prize it open. The wood was extremely old and splintered around the iron lock.

"Papers?" Saul blew dust away and stared in disgust at the contents. "That's all that's in here? Just old papers? What a waste!"

Joseph was about to slam the lid shut when Rachel placed her hand on his shoulder to stop him.

He looked up at her. "What is it?"

"Joseph, things are not always as they appear. Let me take a look at some of these papers."

Saul pushed forward and tapped his homemade bow against the top of Joseph's head and sniggered, "Yeah, Little John, let Maid Marian see if she can decipher the secret documents!"

Rachel rolled her eyes at Saul. She reached in and removed one of the scrolls. Carefully grasping one end, she slowly unrolled it, "Joseph, shine your light on this so I can read it."

Rachel began to silently read to herself. After a few seconds she said, "Hey, do you guys know what these are? Saul, you may've been right."

"Of course I'm right. I'm always right! Wait—what am I right about?"

"These are historical documents. And there's no telling how old they really are. They could go all the way back to—" Rachel suddenly stopped talking.

"What? What is it?"

"Well, I'm not sure. There's a couple of references to a king here," she said.

"To King Richard the Lionhearted!" Saul exclaimed. "One for all and all for one!" he shouted.

"That was the Three Musketeers, Saul. Not Robin Hood," snapped Rachel.

Saul bent down and tightened his bow string. "Yes, well, quite right you are Rachel. Good show," he replied in a fake accent.

"It just looks like a bunch of scribbling to me. How can you read it?" asked Joseph.

Rachel looked up. "I'll have you know there are a lot of things I can do Joseph!" Turning back to the paper, Rachel squinted in concentration. "I haven't seen writing like this since my grandfather read to me. He had an old storybook that he used to read from. It was written in the same way. He told me it was Aramaic. But this—this looks a little more like Phoenician script. Anyway, he taught me how to read it before he died."

"Well, what does it say?" asked Joseph.

"If you will give me a minute I can figure it out," she said patiently. Rachel sat down in front of the chest and continued to read. She read to herself at first, until Saul prodded her enough times with the end of his bow that she gave in and read aloud. She had just about finished reading the one she was holding when they heard a faint noise off in the distance.

"What was that?" asked Joseph. Saul quickly turned and headed for the door. As he stood in the doorway he exclaimed, "I know! It's our villainous foe, the sheriff of Nottingham." And with that Saul turned and ran out of the small chamber. Joseph and Rachel looked at each other and laughed.

"That Saul, he has a one track mind, it's a good thing he has awhile before he needs to worry about saving any *real* kingdoms." said Rachel.

"I think he'd do all right," Joseph laughed.

"It doesn't matter. Let's go. We can come back to our 'chamber of truth' tomorrow. It's getting late and I need to get home."

She put the papers back inside the trunk and Joseph closed the lid. He stood and then reached down and took Rachel's hand to help her up. She gazed into his face as she rose.

"*Merci, mon amour,*" she breathed.

"What did you say?"

"Don't you like it? It's French. My grandmother always said it was a beautiful language."

"Well, what does it mean?"

"Nothing much," she said. "It was just my way of thanking you—my love!" Immediately Joseph could feel his face turning red. He didn't know what to say. He just looked at Rachel and smiled.

"What did you call this place? The Chamber of Truth?" he asked.

"Yes, it has a nice ring to it, don't you think?"

Joseph listened to the quiet of the cave. "I wonder where Saul is."

"He's probably fighting with his shadow. You know what a sucker he is for adventure."

"I'm gonna go see if I can find him. Can you find your way back to the main door?"

"Of course I can, but it would be much better if you would walk me," Rachel said with the hint of a smile. Joseph reached in his pocket and took out his flashlight and turned it on. "Here," he said, thrusting it at her. "You can use this. I'll meet you outside." Rachel sighed and took the light.

"Okay. Go on. But you better be waiting for me when I get up there, Joseph Zeigler. I mean it! You know it'll be dark soon."

"I know, I know. I'll be there," he said, as he disappeared into the darkness.

Rachel spent a few more minutes in the chamber before she started for home. She managed to find her way back up to the great hall without any difficulty. As she neared the entrance she could see that it was late and it had started to snow. Knowing that she needed to get home she ran up the steps that led to the main doorway and the exit. Just as she was about to step through the door she caught a glimpse of a silhouette hidden in the shadows. She turned to the shadowy figure and said, "Joseph, are you going to just stand there, or are you going to walk me home?"

"Just once it might be nice to surprise you. How did you know it was me?" Joseph asked, stepping in to the light of the doorway.

"Please, are you kidding me?" asked Rachel. "Who else would it be? Now are you going to walk me home or am I going to have to walk up this snow-covered mountain by myself?"

From out of the darkness an arrow sprang and struck the door frame above their heads. "Step away from the fair maiden, Little John," echoed the voice from the depths of the stairwell.

Rachel turned and looked back down the steps, her face flushed with anger. "Saul, I don't have time for this! I've got to get home!"

"That's Sir Robin to you, my fair lady," sniffed Saul. Rachel looked at Joseph and rolled her eyes.

"You know Saul, you're getting a bit too close with those arrows. One of these days you're gonna kill one of us," she said.

Saul stepped in to the light. He was wearing an archer's hat, a green suede tunic over a white shirt, and green tights with boots. He removed his hat with a flourish and bowed, "I am at your service, M'lady. Is this person hindering you from embarking on your journey?"

"No Saul, that would be you. You're hindering me. I've got to get home before it gets dark," Rachel said with determination.

"Well then, I bid you farewell. Take care of her, Achi!" Saul commanded.

"As you wish, my prince," answered Joseph solemnly.

Rachel shook her head, "You two are unbelievable."

"Ah, come on Rachel, we are just having some fun!" said Joseph. And, with that, he stepped through the door and escorted her outside, waving to Saul, "See you tomorrow!"

Saul cupped his hand and yelled, "Remember, not a word to anyone about the treasure!"

As Joseph walked Rachel up the mountain, Saul sealed the entryway to the cavern. Continuing up the snowy path, Rachel told Joseph she'd finally figured out what was written on the papers.

"What?" Joseph asked.

With a mischievous grin she stopped in the middle of the trail, hitched up her shirt in the back and slipped her hand inside her skirt. Joseph could see that she was holding one of the old parchment papers.

"Rachel, what are you doing? Saul told us to keep this a secret!"

"How is he going to find out? Are you going to tell him?" asked Rachel with a raised brow.

Joseph's head dropped. "No, I'm not going to say a word. But I'll get blamed for it if this goes badly—just you wait and see."

Rachel gave him a quick kiss on the cheek.

For a moment Joseph was stunned, "What did you do that for?"

"*Vous êtes mon meilleur ami et je t'aime*," said Rachel shyly before she turned and ran up the trail.

"Hey, what's that supposed to mean? You know I can't speak French!"

He touched his cheek where Rachel had kissed him. It was the first time that he'd been kissed by anyone other than his mother. And this wasn't anything like that. Joseph's face lit up, and he took off running after her. The light dusting of snow made the trail slippery and his feet slid with every step. Trying to maintain his balance, he called out, "Hey, Rachel! Wait up!"

Outskirts of Jerusalem—Twenty-five Years Later

Joseph jerked awake and placed a hand to his cheek. It hadn't been a dream; it had been a memory, he was sure of it. The details were already fading as he tried to reconstruct the images that had run through his head. Shaking his head, he rubbed his temples as the particulars faded into the darkness.

Putting in eleven- to twelve-hour days had started to take its toll. He had been at his desk since six that morning, and as he looked over the blueprints, it was hard to keep his eyes open. It had been a long week and he was beginning to feel the exhaustion. The first few times he'd managed to shake himself awake, but finally he drifted off to sleep. He'd dreamed. The dream was vivid. In it, his childhood friends Rachel and Saul were playing with him in some place that seemed very familiar. It was a great hall. They were all young, about eleven or twelve years old. The three of them played as Robin Hood, Little John, and Maid

Marian. Then, as Rachel was leaving to return home for the evening, she'd kissed him, and as she took off running, he'd yelled after her and chased her through the snow. It was the first memory he was sure of since he'd been treated after his service in the Israeli Army.

It was almost dark when Joseph finished looking over the newly revised plans for the temple. He'd really been pushing it since they finally got the security diagrams back from the architectural firm; he'd been able to look through most of them before it started to get dark. He rolled the documents up and placed them on top of one of the oak file cabinets next to his desk. Joseph watched the roll of papers rock back and forth in the cabinet until they finally came to a rest. Staring at the diagrams, there was an eerie feeling of déjà vu. He couldn't put his finger on it. They looked a little like some old documents he'd once seen, maybe in a picture or on TV, he didn't know.

The alarm on his watch chimed the seven o'clock hour. It was time for him to head back to the city. Tomorrow's forecast was sunny with a high of sixty-seven degrees. The weather was unusually warm for this time of year. Joseph's day had been long, and he looked forward to having a couple of days off. He planned to meet up with a couple of old friends. He checked the time again and did the mental calculations on travel; if he left now he could make it back to the city in time to change.

Almost a year had passed since he'd been able to get together with his friends. He looked forward to it. As he finished tidying up his desk, Joseph walked over to the window to see if anybody was still around. His was the only car remaining in the parking lot. He checked the side lot and found it too was empty. It appeared that everyone had already left the compound for the weekend. He pulled out his cell phone and hit the quick dial to call the Royal Palace with his thumb. *What a surprise, no bars and no service.* Joseph shook his head. *This whole area is a dead zone.* He reached down and turned off the radio sitting on his desk and headed down the stairs.

As Joseph began walking down the steps, he heard a bang that sounded like gunfire. The sound echoed through the empty site as Joseph listened. *A car backfiring.* Years in the military had taught him the difference, but years in a land in constant conflict had taught him caution. As Joseph arrived at the main floor, he decided to use the Porta John before hitting the road. After walking outside, he stopped at the first one and made a survey of the corners, inside and out by the vents. It was a ritual he was now in the habit of doing ever since he found out that he was allergic to wasps.

Making sure it was all clear, he stepped inside and closed the door. No cell towers, no pest control, and no running water or electricity beyond what the generators could provide. He thought about how great it would be once construction got a little further along. As he stood over the small urinal, Joseph heard shuffling outside. He called out, announcing that he'd be out in a minute. After finishing up, he opened the door and stepped back out into the compound. The site was empty. He looked back toward the main building, puzzled. Shaking his head, he headed for the parking lot, and again thought he heard something moving near the south gate.

"Hello, is there someone there?"

No response. Maybe it was one of the guards. Arriving at the south gate he checked inside the gatehouse—empty. He called out for the guards. No answer. *Where were those guys?* Joseph tried to remember the gatehouse hours. He had seen the schedule. The gates would be manned weekdays until six. He checked his watch again. It was already a little past seven. *Terrific. The guards have already left.*

An eerie feeling settled in. In a flash, a shadow detached itself from the shadows by the guard station and jumped out, grabbing hold of his collar and shouting. The man pushed him backwards. He had a heavy accent and was wearing some kind of dark-colored head wrap that covered most of his face.

Joseph tensed for a fight. His five-foot-ten-inch frame was solid muscle, a leftover from days spent working in the quarry. As the man shoved Joseph again, something caught his foot and he stumbled to the ground. He bounced back to his feet, and the attacker caught him with a weak jab in the face and called him by name.

"Joseph! Give us the soul! We know you have it. I will kill you if you don't give it!" he screamed. It was English. It was barely intelligible through his harsh accent, but Joseph recognized the language.

Joseph made one last attempt to reply, but as he opened his mouth a second jab smashed into his throat. He was knocked to the ground again. The wind knocked out of him, he lay there, dazed and gasping for breath before passing out.

Blinking awake, Joseph slowly stood. He felt blinded, and he knew his throat was bruised. He stumbled around, trying to get his bearings. *Where am I? What the hell just happened?* He couldn't have been out but a few minutes; the sun was still sinking over the horizon. He began to walk toward what he thought was the parking lot. As Joseph rounded a corner, he was floored by a gut-punch that winded him. Then he heard the shouting. "Give them to us you god damned fool!" It was the same command, but came from a different voice.

"What the hell do you want?" He must have been out just long enough for the first to go get help. Whoever these thugs were, they were persistent. The second attacker's breath reeked of cheap wine. Grabbing his arm the man swung Joseph around like a rag doll, but his hands slipped and Joseph jerked away and took off running. *Who in the hell are these guys? What do they want?*

Joseph ran back across the compound, toward an opening in the partially constructed temple wall. As Joseph neared it, he stumbled over a piece of partially cut stone and fell again, biting his tongue. He could taste the blood in his mouth, and he knew his throat was starting to swell. His tongue felt thick and everything was spinning. Blood dripped on his shirt, from a nasty cut under his chin.

Dragging himself upright, he headed toward the west gate. Dark was really setting in now; he leaned against one of the large pillars that the workmen had set up on the front porch of the main building. The pillar was smooth and cold to the touch. Each one had been cut from the finest Parian marble and quarried from the Greek Island of Paros before being hauled up the river on barges.

The pillar helped steady him for the moment, and he regained his focus. He had to stop and try to catch his breath. As he leaned against it, a feeling of familiarity came over him. He remembered as a young boy playing around such gigantic columns as he ran and chased his friends. Shaking himself in an attempt to remain lucid he tried to force the memory to the side while he focused on the world around him. There was nothing—no weapons, or at least nothing on the construction site he could lift and maneuver. Keeping to his refuge behind the structure, Joseph tried to be as still and quiet as possible. He tried to listen, but his heart was beating so loudly that it was difficult for him to hear anyone approach. Even his attackers could probably hear its throbbing.

He had to figure out his next move. He needed to get someone's attention. But who was there to hear him? *Was anyone here?* The construction workers had taken off for the day. He knew the guards usually tried to keep the east gate open until the last vehicle had left, so that was his best chance.

As Joseph inched his way toward the gate, he called out to the guards in a hoarse whisper. He raised the volume of his voice as he called again. No answer.

When he finally reached the gatehouse it was empty. He pulled out his cell again, hoping for better luck. Just as he opened the phone, strong hands grabbed him from behind. The phone went flying. Joseph managed a quick jab to the man's jaw, or would have if he had been a head shorter. This guy was big, much bigger than the other two. Two massive arms grabbed Joseph and held him still, and as he struggled, a bag was rammed over Joseph's head. It was some kind of rasping cloth, and light powder was falling over his face as he struggled, getting into his nose and mouth. Then the shouting resumed.

"Just give it to us, we don't want to hurt you!" Joseph recognized the voice as coming from the man who first attacked him. They were all together now, and the three ruffians bound Joseph's hands with rope and tightened the sack around his neck. He felt as if he were suffocating. He'd never felt so powerless in his life.

Having heard Joseph calling out to the guards, one of the men mocked him. "The guards have all left for the day. All you have is me. What are you going to do now?" he snarled.

Another cut him off. "All we want is the soul, give it to us and we will be done with you! Just cooperate and everything will be fine." Joseph tried to nod at this, but the sack over his head obscured his movements. A heavy blow landed on his cheek, and he felt the warmth of blood as the harsh bag cut his jaw.

"What is more important to you, huh? Your life or your king? The soul you fool!"

They were all speaking English—who were they? Joseph had no idea what they were talking about. *The king, something to do with the king.* He wasn't in any shape to make more sense than that, but it was all he needed. Joseph could feel his body getting weaker, but he managed to shake his head; he knew he was losing a lot of blood. He felt his legs starting to buckle and was afraid he might be losing consciousness again. As Joseph began to lose his strength and footing, two of the men stabilized him. Joseph spit out the blood pooling in his mouth; it stuck to the bag, turning it red.

A sudden pain cut into his back; they were whipping him! He was weak, but suddenly enraged. *How dare they? Who the hell are these people?* The pain gripped him, but his anger gave him precious time of clarity. The only way he was going to get out of this alive was to give his captors what they wanted. He had to figure out what that was.

"Get the hell off me! What do you want!" lashing out with his limbs he felt his leg and elbow connect. But it was just a small victory—he suddenly felt a sudden brilliance of pain in his nose and heard his own neck pop as his head flew back against his spine. Blackness was all that was left.

Icy cold water splashed across his face. He had no idea how long he'd been out. He was being dragged, gravel and grass ground into his back as they dragged him by his feet through a small creek. His arms were still tightly bound, and except for the sack on his head most of his clothes had been torn away. Joseph could feel the cold air off the mountain. The cold creek water had revived him, but he knew it wouldn't last long. *Damn them! They're going to kill me for sure! What the hell do they want from me?*

When his captors pulled him up onto the creek bank, he felt as though he were under water, and his senses ignored his commands to run. "Just leave!" he begged. "Just leave me, please!" He listened as they made plans of how they were going to dispose of his body, bury it beyond the outskirts of town, and then get out of the country.

Joseph began to feel his life slipping away, felt the dulling grip of death on his body. Silently, he gave his last thoughts to his Creator. *Oh Lord, my God is there no help for the widow's son?* Without another thought, he slipped into the darkness.

2

Joseph's eyes fluttered open as consciousness slowly returned, and with it the pain registering in every inch of his body. The world was dark. *Is it still night?* he wondered. The air was stuffy, and cloth fluttered against his dry lips with each breath, leaving the taste of flour. The bag was still over his head. His weak attempt to remove it told him that his hands were still tied, and even that simple effort exhausted him.

He had no idea how long he'd been out, and for a time it was all he could do to lie still and try to sort through the memories that flooded his mind. He had been attacked, in the compound, as he was leaving. *Those bastards.* Slowly, his senses were returning, and with them a new fear as Joseph heard chattering voices around him. He froze, his eyes snapping open within the confines of the bag as adrenaline awakened clarity once more. He tried to make out what they were saying. *Are the attackers still here?* It was a group of people, how many he couldn't tell. Their voices came from every direction, rasping and yelling in his ears, and he couldn't make out a single word. Joseph took a shallow breath and focused his mind. They must have seen him move; they must know he was awake. He would have to make a run for it. Joseph set his jaw, and felt his stomach tighten as he prepared for one last chance at freedom. *Please God, help your child!*

Before he could rise, something heavy landed on his head causing particles of flour to fall and burn his eyes. Sharp needles bit slowly into his scalp, and something screeched into his ear. Whatever landed on him was now industriously picking at the bag over his head causing even more particles to cascade into his face, coating his eyelashes. *What the hell is going on?* Shaking the thing off Joseph rolled to his knees as voices rose angrily around him. In fervor, he worked off the leather restraints, rubbing his skin raw, until the last loop of the rope fell away and ripped the sack off his head as he rose. Instantly, he was blinded as the midday sunlight shone into his eyes causing him to misstep and fall once again to the soggy earth.

Sucking in his first lungful of air free of the sack, his body quickly tried to retch it back out as the taste of salt and filth coated his tongue. All around him was a sea of garbage, and a few paces away a seagull looked on, clearly irritated to find Joseph still alive, before taking off to join the hundreds of other scavengers that dotted the sky of the landfill. It took a moment to realize where he was; the dump was just around the rear of the compound.

His wrists felt unfamiliar. A pale shadow on his otherwise tan skin showed vividly against his irritated, raw flesh. One of those guys had stolen his watch. He looked at his wrist and could see where the band had scraped the top of his hand as it had been wrenched off. Joseph let out a long, drawn out scream that faded quickly in the open air. He knew it was irrational, he knew he should be thankful to be alive, but anger filled every inch of him as he sat, alone, insulted, cast aside in a garbage heap.

The watch had been a gift—a gift from the king—and Joseph wanted it back. He was not looking forward to breaking the news of its disappearance. King Oman had given him two rules to follow as a contract for accepting the gift: the first was to never lose the watch, and the second was to remember the first. The watch had a royal blue dial and was surrounded by forty round-cut diamonds held on by an 18K yellow gold band and faceplate. Its net worth had been sixteen thousand American dollars. As he stood, he felt a tingling sensation in his toes. They had gone to sleep. He was also well aware of the pounding sensation in his head. He didn't know what they'd hit him with, but from the aftermath it had probably been a sledgehammer. Looking over his almost naked form he realized the watch wasn't all that had been taken. They'd left him his boxers and his sandals. Judging by the cuts and scratches that ran the length of his body he'd probably been dragged *after* his clothes had been removed. His chest was a mass of drying blood where deep cuts crisscrossed just below his neck. Grimacing, he surveyed the area and tried to clear his mind.

If his memory of the facility's blueprints served him correctly, he was only about three or four hundred meters from where he had first been assaulted near the south gate. Looking toward the compound, images of the fight flashed through his head. His cell had been knocked from his hands not too far from here. *Where was that?* As Joseph rose to his feet he tried to retrace his steps. His search was fruitless. *They must have taken that too.* Tucking the sack cloth into his waistband he limped back to the parking lot to get his car. He didn't have keys, but Israeli military service had taught him ways around that. As he arrived in the garage, Joseph stopped in an empty parking lot. For a moment all he felt was the dead weight of his circumstances before anger again rose from his stomach. "YOU BASTARDS!" His yell echoed off the garage walls.

Joseph walked around the entire complex to see if any service vehicles had been parked on site; even a golf cart would be welcome, but he found nothing. All of the vehicles had been used to transport the workers back to the city. The security guards were gone, all the workers had been ferried out, and he'd been attacked just when he'd gotten off work. He had no cell phone, no watch, no clothes, and now, no car. He wasn't sure what was going on, but he needed help. A walk around the compound didn't reveal even a carpenter's apron to cover him. Without clothes and without a way to get back to the city, Joseph started walking down the long stretch of road.

Every mile or so, Joseph was forced to spit out the blood and scab that continually found their way into his mouth, and the throbbing in his head made his steps waver. A quick probe of his face revealed a cut along his cheek and swelling above his nose, which hurt too much to touch. He didn't really remember getting hit, but it must have been what had knocked him out. After making his way across the landfill, Joseph came upon a small creek.

He didn't know if it was the same one that his attackers had dragged him through or not. He knelt down near the edge of the cool trickling water and scooped up some of the clear liquid with his hands and took a drink. The cold water was sweet solace as it made its way down his throat. Scooping up more he let it trickle down his face and legs, chilling his swollen skin. Finally, the world had given him a reprieve, however slight, and he felt the tears forming beneath his closed eyes. He almost missed the scuffling of dirt behind him, alerting him of someone's presence.

With more energy than he knew he had, Joseph spun around and found himself ready to leap at a small donkey staring him in the face. Off balance, Joseph fell back, landing in the creek with a small splash. The donkey just stared as his boxers quickly filled with water. Scooping up a palm full of water, he flung it in the animal's face. The donkey didn't flinch or move as Joseph continued to drink. It just kept looking at him with its big brown eyes.

"Good morning to you, my four-legged friend. You wouldn't happen to know what time it is would you?"

The donkey made a couple of braying noises before walking past Joseph and disappearing into the countryside.

"No, I didn't think so." Joseph took a few moments to wash out his wounds. His chest was a mass of cuts, but he cleaned out the caked mud and grime as best he could.

The blood didn't bother him—he'd been through worse. In fact, he was often amazed he'd lived as long as he had. He'd survive. The first thing he needed to do was to find some clothes. Walking naked into town might raise . . . issues. And, he needed to get help. Whoever had tried to kill him would return, and they would have one thing on their minds: getting rid of the body they thought was still lying in a garbage heap.

3

As Joseph leaned down for one last drink from the creek a small silver chain became untangled from around his neck, and a small bauble swung like a pendulum to hang before his eyes; it hovered just over the water. Sitting upright on his knees he grasped the chain and examined the carving. He was astounded that it had not been torn off during the struggle. It must have become tangled around his neck when they'd pulled the sack over his head. As Joseph straightened the chain, he smirked with delight and satisfaction.

The jewel had been given to Joseph as a token of appreciation from the king for all the work that he'd done at the palace. As a young boy, Joseph had become interested in being a metal smith. Like many boys, he had been drawn to follow in his father's footsteps. And, like his father, Joseph specialized in working with copper, tin, and brass. When he began his apprenticeship, he was interested in molding and shaping the metals into different forms and patterns. As he continued to advance, he obtained his license as a Journeyman. He took on more and more complex projects and, within several years, established himself as a respected businessman and a master craftsman. Joseph's reputation and talent led to the king taking more of an interest in his work. The king was King Saul Oman.

The king had been Joseph's best and closest friend since they were both small boys, back when the king had been a prince and Joseph simply called him Saul. Although, in their adventures they had taken on many other names: Tom and Huck, Athos and Porthos, David and Goliath, and Robin Hood and Little John. Many people who did not know the young boys had thought they were brothers. And in a way they were.

Joseph's father, Ethan, had supported himself and Joseph with his skill in metal and wood carving. In fact Ethan had become so skillful with his hands that he was commissioned by Saul's father, King Caro, to build a special anniversary cedar chest for the Queen. Ethan never had to work for anyone else again. He had become the king's most trusted servant and worked exclusively for the royal family. Eventually he had specialized in creating safes and vaults, guarding the royal family's most precious valuables. Saul and Joseph became even closer. The palace was also where they met Rachel.

Rachel's mother, Devorah, also worked for the royal family. She was the queen's social secretary. However, when she first started working at the palace she'd been the queen's head seamstress. She seemed to work magic with a needle. She created all of the queen's gowns, social apparel, and her riding habits and sportswear. Rachel enjoyed the artistic benefits that her mother created for her in the royal sewing room, always having beautiful clothes, even as a child. Her mother had drilled grooming habits and skills into her head from the time she was old enough to brush her teeth, and she made sure her daughter could measure up to the best dressed and the most meticulously groomed socialite. This was quite a feat because money had often been tight in their household. Having to be at the royal family's disposal at all hours of the day and night, their staff's living quarters were set up in the main building, near the royal residence. Saul, Joseph, and Rachel took full advantage of this and just like their fictional American counterparts Tom, Huck, and Becky, they became inseparable.

Working directly for the king had other advantages too. For one it allowed Joseph to travel around the country. With Saul, he saw the great works of their country and even those around the world. He saw works of master craftsmen when he was a child that many could only read about.

Joseph let the jewel in his hand drop back around his neck. It was very old. In fact, Saul had obtained the jewel many years before from one of the king's old temple guards. Fashioned out of gold and silver, it was shaped to resemble a plumb, one of the working tools of Joseph's trade.

His body didn't let him enjoy his find for long, as a pain in his stomach reminded him that water would not satiate the gnawing in his stomach. He was fatigued, and needed food and rest. For what remained of the morning, Joseph walked along the road, foraging pistachios and pomegranates that he found along the way.

After an eternity, he found himself in the outskirts of the Holy City. Collapsing in the shade of the brush and trees a few paces off the roadway, he decided to hide near the edge of a small cemetery to give him a few minutes to try to form a plan. From the position of the sun, Joseph figured that it was about one or two o'clock; he would have a long wait if he wanted to enter the city in darkness to avoid embarrassment, and possible arrest. The soft crunch of feet against gravel warned him that someone was approaching, and he hunkered farther into the brush.

A few moments later, a small funeral procession began to make its way to the cemetery. From Joseph's vantage point, he counted seven people walking in a slow and somber stride, one behind the other. An elderly rabbi led the procession reading from the Torah, his mouth twisting beneath a grayed beard. As the funeral procession grew closer, Joseph could hear the prayers being sung and drifting over the cemetery. A two-wheeled cart, pulled by a single donkey and followed by grievers, contained a simple wooden coffin. Two burly pallbearers ended the procession, their eyes watching the ground, and one wiped tears from his face. Joseph had seen it all far too many times. He remembered standing at the side of the grave for his friends in the military, murmuring prayers into the soft earth, and again for a friend gunned down in Tel Aviv by anti gay activists, and again for his father. The memory of seeing his father for the last time brought tears to his eyes as the prayers filled his ears and heart.

As the procession arrived at the gravesite, the two pallbearers took hold of the coffin and carried it from the wagon, lowering it carefully with ropes into the grave as the rabbi sang the Kaddish, a mourning prayer. Joseph watched as one of the women, in a headscarf and shawl, discreetly tore the left side of her blouse. He knew and understood the significance. Sadly, he realized that the deceased must have been her child. As the service ended, the seven mourners took turns with the shovel, each throwing three shovelfuls of dirt into the grave, and made their way back down the path.

Watching the mourners leave, Joseph had an idea. He tried to ignore it—it seemed irrelevant—but the thought persisted, almost as if it were being whispered in his ear. He couldn't help it—the thoughts began unfolding in his mind, quickly making connections, and molding themselves into a plan. Maybe, with a little help here, he could figure out why all of this had happened. As the last mourner had walked away from the gravesite Joseph saw that one of the men was walking with the woman who had torn her blouse. Their affection for each other was obvious, and Joseph whispered a soft prayer and thanks to them and their family. The only remaining member of the procession was an older gentleman who immediately started covering the coffin with the fresh mound of dirt that had been piled up alongside the grave.

It is said, the lord will guide our path, Joseph thought. *Please guide me now.* As the man continued to shovel the dirt into the grave, Joseph managed to make his way a little closer using the brush to conceal his movements.

Joseph spoke. "Your ceremony was proper and your grief was true." When Joseph began to speak, it startled the old man who glanced around and quickly dropped to his knees, bowing his head to the ground. Seeing no one, the old man believed that some kind of spirit or angel had spoken to him. For a moment Joseph broke, wanting only to help the man rise. But, the voice whispered again and he hardened his resolve. Again he spoke, "What is it that you seek, Achi?"

As the old gentleman continued to kneel, his voice was soft and frail. The words that he spoke were barely audible. However, he understood what the old gentleman said when he whispered, "*Ain Svp Avr.*"

Joseph was surprised to hear the old Jewish reference.

Joseph answered, "What you seek shall someday be yours, but today is not that day. You must wait until it is your time. Your work is not yet done. You have much more light to receive, Achi."

His voice still shook as he spoke. "What then can I do to please the One who is speaking to me from the grave?"

Joseph bit his lip. "Return to your family. Now is the time that they will need your wisdom and your strength."

The old man rose to his feet and left the cemetery without looking back, leaving the shovel, and without the donkey and cart. When the gentleman had disappeared from sight, Joseph took the shovel and scooped out the loose dirt that had already been thrown on top of the coffin, hoping that the services were for a man and that the man would be close to his size. The coffin had been nailed shut, and he was forced to use the end of his shovel to pry the lid open.

As he slid the lid off of the handcrafted wooden box, he found the body of a young man within. *The poor boy*, Joseph thought. *Cut down in the prime of life. He couldn't be more than twenty-two years old.* The boy's angular features were accented by a small and neatly trimmed mustache and beard. Pulling the shroud away from the body revealed a suit roughly of Joseph's dimensions, and a plain yarmulka adorning his head. Checking the man's pockets, Joseph found a photo I.D. that read *James Pearlman*. Joseph offered a quick prayer thanking him, glad that he knew the young man's name. The head covering was to remind man that there would always be something between him and his Great Creator.

Slowly, he lifted James's frail body up and out of the coffin, surprised at how light the body was. Joseph started to gently remove James's outer garments and expose his fragile remains.

He must have struggled with sickness before the end. Joseph was taught early that what remained within the coffin after the individual had passed away was only a shell that held a person's spirit. As Joseph thought about this, the last thing he did was remove James's kippah. Folding it neatly into a half moon, he placed it back into the coffin. Hopefully he would be able to return James's body back to its final resting place without his family ever knowing what had happened. After Joseph finished getting into James's clothes and slippers, he placed the lid back on the coffin and filled the grave.

4

Joseph patted the top of the grave with the flat of the shovel and sat quietly by the small mound. He thought about all of those wonderful days when he was just a boy and his father would take him to work. He remembered how his father taught him to play the violin when he was around eleven or twelve. It was never one of his talents, but his father never seemed to mind. Ethan loved to play the violin, along with several other stringed instruments. As a boy, Joseph could remember listening to his father play into the early morning hours. Joseph had usually fallen asleep long before his father stopped playing for the evening. The music was like a sweet drug, rendering him unconscious whenever he sat still and tried to focus and listen.

As Joseph grew a little older and became a better musician, his father would let him play along. Those were special times. Thinking back to those days, Joseph wished he could bottle the moments. It had been a long time since Joseph had seen his father. He would never forget that terrible day when he received the news of his father's death.

At the time Joseph was three weeks into basic training with the Israeli Army. He had been summoned to appear before the base rabbi. Joseph was granted permission for emergency leave to return home so he could attend his father's funeral. It was only when he got back to the city that he was told that his father, Ethan, had been murdered. The detective working the case explained to Joseph that his father had been stabbed in the chest while at the synagogue. Of course, that was only after he had been beaten. The autopsy revealed the murder weapon to be a dagger. The hypothesis was that while Ethan was praying someone entered the synagogue, when they knew he'd be alone. There had not been a struggle, but his father had never been a big man. His murderer grabbed him from behind and thrust the dagger's blade deep into Ethan's chest.

There were no suspects or persons of interest identified. The weapon was never found. The only information provided by the police about a possible suspect was that Joseph's father apparently knew his attacker. This was determined by the fact that the assailant apparently knew Ethan's usual customs and daily routine. This person even knew when Ethan was going to pray. Although the detective working the case vowed that he would never give up the hunt, the case had remained unsolved.

No matter how successful Joseph could become, he thought that he would never come close to being the man that his father had been. Sometimes, it bothered him that they were so different and other times he knew, in his heart, that their differences were a blessing. Joseph found himself blinking back tears. There were no pure memories anymore; everything was colored by violence and loss. It was then that he wished for that bottle, so he could pop it open and relive a more innocent time.

As he stood, he realized that James's clothes were just a little bit tight, but it was a far cry from running around the countryside in his underwear. The next step in the plan would be trickier. If his plan was going to work, he had to make sure that the illusion of his demise continued for just a little while longer. Maybe then he could find out who had attacked him and who was really responsible for trying to overthrow the king. Joseph had to stop and think for a moment. Was that what this was really all about? Was someone really trying to overthrow the king or was it something a little more personal? Granted, it would not be the first time that it had been tried. Is this what is happening now? Joseph shook the thought from his head; now wasn't the time to jump to conclusions. He could deal with those questions when he met with the king.

Checking the position of the sun once again, Joseph decided that it was time for him to get moving. Wrapping James's body back in the white sheet and laying him on the cart, he hoped he wouldn't run into anyone who might want to ask a lot of questions. Making the nine- to ten-kilometer journey from the cemetery back to the compound, Joseph found himself talking to the donkey, along the way deciding that the animal needed a name. After running through a dozen or so, Joseph decided that he would call him Pegasus. It wasn't because the donkey could, so much, fly like the wind. More particularly, it was because the donkey broke a lot of wind.

Rounding a bend on the old logging road that led back to the compound, Joseph pulled back on the halter and Pegasus came to a stop. Now he knew why Saul had chosen this particular location for the new temple. Looking toward the temple's dome sitting atop a skeletal frame, Joseph knew this would be a magnificent structure once it was finally completed. Seeing the blueprints and looking at the real thing was a world of difference. Reluctantly, Joseph snapped the halter, and he and Pegasus continued their journey until they drew near where Joseph had been left by his captors.

Carefully picking James up in his arms, Joseph carried him to the garbage heap. Joseph made every effort to position the young man in the exact spot where they had left him. He even tossed some dirt and other rubbish on and around James so that it would appear as though the body had been dragged from the temple. After taking the sack cloth and pulling it over James's head, he slipped his sandals off and onto James's feet. Hopefully, the ruffians would be in such a hurry to get rid of the body they wouldn't take the time to remove the sack.

Turning to leave, something caught against his throat, metallic and thin. His necklace had become caught on a button on the coat. Moving to untangle it, an idea surfaced. It was like another voice in his ear. The jewel had a microchip embedded within it. Afraid he might lose a gift from the king, Joseph had it embedded years ago. Then it wouldn't matter where the ruffians took the body. With a prayer, he looped the jewel around the boy's neck. All that needed to be done was to activate the tracking system and let the microchip locate the body. For a moment he paused, ready to reach back out and take Saul's token of friendship back with him, but again the idea whispered itself in his ear.

With a sigh, Joseph pulled the sack cloth over the jewel and chain, concealing it from view. When he finished staging the scene, he took Pegasus and the cart to the opposite end of the compound and into the woods, tying them to a tree. Returning to the temple compound, he retrieved a pair of binoculars from one of the cabinets in his office. The door had been locked, but at this point that wasn't stopping him. When this got settled, he'd pay for the damages. Climbing up to the second story of the main building he found a good vantage point where he could keep watch over James's body.

As the sun finally dropped behind the mountains, darkness settled in and fatigue finally took hold. He wasn't just tired, he was totally exhausted. Slowly, the drudgery of his clandestine surveillance got the best of him. He tried to keep his eyes open, but his body's needs took hold. Just before he dozed off, he remembered thinking about his three assailants, and questions filled his dreams: *Who are these guys? What were they after? How did they know me?*

5

Joseph hadn't been asleep long when he started to dream. In his dreams he was back in the quarry, working, once again a teenager. Joseph's father had persuaded the overseer to let him work weekends so that he could get some experience. His dream took him back to his first day on the job, the overseer showing him around and introducing him to some of the other workers.

One in particular was an acquaintance from school. His face was familiar, but it shifted in and out of recognition. This guy instantly took a liking to Joseph and, after a while, he'd been invited to join his fellow workman and a couple younger brothers after work. On one such occasion the older brother excused himself and told Joseph that he needed to leave to attend a lodge meeting. He had recalled his father saying something similar to his mother about attending lodge. Joseph asked him what kind of lodge meeting he had attended and fragments of their conversation floated back to him. It had been his first introduction to the Masons.

"Hasn't your father talked to you about the lodge?"

"No, you know how that generation is. Everything is so secretive."

Joseph's friend had laughed. "Oh how true" he said. "I'll tell you what Joseph, if you're interested, I can get you a petition. Being a Lewis, that means your father is a Mason, so you're almost assured to get in. You are eighteen aren't you?"

"Yes, I'm eighteen, but how did you know my father is a Mason?"

The man winked at Joseph. "He was at lodge last evening. Brother Ethan asked me how you were doing in the quarry. I told him you were doing fine and that I thought you would make a good Mason."

"What did he say when you told him that?" Joseph asked.

"He told me that the lodge could use another good man." This was the first time that Joseph's father had referred to him as a *man*. Even in his dream, Joseph remembered the pride he had felt.

Joseph's friend had become his tutor, and in his sleep Joseph murmured the *catechism* they had worked on so many times together. After work he and Joseph would find a quiet place to study. Joseph found it interesting that although his friend could not read, he was quite proficient in instruction. Finally during one November evening, Joseph gave his final catechism and became a Master Mason. It was quite an event, and the small lodge hall was packed. Joseph had been surprised to see many of his father's friends in attendance. Joseph was even more surprised once the blindfold had been removed to see Saul extending his right hand and elevating him to the Sublime Degree of Master Mason. It was a night that Joseph would never forget. For a time, Joseph discovered that this new relationship with his lodge brother filled a void that had been vacated when Saul had ascended to the throne as king.

However, shortly after becoming a Master Mason, Joseph was inducted into the military. All young men became part of the Israeli Army when they reach their eighteenth birthday. Just before Joseph began his basic training in the northern Negev desert region, he learned that his friend and lodge brother would not be following him.

"It's the tests." Joseph could see his face perfectly captured, and the shame he had tried to hide in turning away. "I did pretty well when it came to the physical part, but when it came to taking tests, I just didn't have a clue. They told me I have some 'learning disability.' I told them I just couldn't read the damn questions."

"It's their loss, my friend" Joseph replied. "I will forever be grateful to you for being my teacher and friend. I will never forget you, Shor."

Joseph's eyes opened wide, and for a moment the name lingered in his ear. "Shor," he whispered, "I sure wish you could have been with me today. We would have shown those boys at the compound a thing or two."

Looking around, Joseph realized that it had gotten completely dark. *How long have I been asleep?* Suddenly, he heard a noise from beyond the window near the garbage site. He quickly grabbed his binoculars and started looking out towards the rubbish. At first, all he saw was blackness, but soon he picked up movement near where he laid James's body. He quickly focused the binoculars on a couple of scavenging hyenas scurrying around in the garbage, looking for something to eat.

He picked up a small piece of sheetrock from the floor and hurled it at the dogs. "GET OUT OF HERE!" he shouted. Hooting, the animals retreated to a safe distance. He managed to zoom in on a couple of rats playing with a piece of bread, and watched as a snake lurked about, searching for a midnight snack, and on mosquitoes. There were thousands of mosquitoes buzzing in the night, turning what little light there was into the illusion of static. There were so many of them that they formed a small, dark cloud over the garbage. Joseph had just about decided to call it quits when he heard what sounded like a gunshot just beyond the ridge near the service road.

Quickly, Joseph refocused his binoculars. He looked just in time to see a couple of headlights coming down the road. Through the binoculars, Joseph could see it was an old truck, maybe a Dodge. He guessed it to be a nineteen sixty-three or sixty-four model. The left headlamp kept blinking on and off with each bump. As the truck got a little closer, Joseph was able to count three individuals inside, two sitting up front in the cab and one in the back, in the bed. Getting closer still, he could see that there was rust all along the top of the hood and cab. It certainly didn't look like any service vehicle returning to the site.

As the old truck pulled to a stop there was another backfire that triggered Joseph's memory. He remembered a similar sound just before he had been assaulted the day before. *Welcome back.* The guy riding in the back hopped out and walked up to the driver's side window; it looked as though they were talking. Joseph regretted not scoping out a location closer. After a few more minutes he watched as the two men in the cab got out and walked to the back and retrieved some sort of tarp or canvas.

Walking up the embankment toward the landfill, they entered the temple grounds and made their way toward the rear of the property. Joseph watched for another ten or fifteen minutes as they meandered around, faint whispers of voices reaching his perch, as they looked for the body. One gave a shout and waved his hand as the other two hustled over. Kneeling down, they spread the canvas tarp out, rolled the body up and tied it off. *They didn't check the sack, at least not yet.* Two of them hoisted the tarp up on their shoulders—an awkward affair as the one in the front was about a head taller and twice the width in muscle—and headed back down the trail towards the truck. The third led the way with the lantern.

Arriving back at the truck, the two guys who were carrying the body tossed it into the bed. The biggest man paused, speaking to the other two before getting into the driver's seat. Joseph figured that he must be the man who had caused his bruised nose. Starting the engine of the old Dodge, the driver ground the gears several times before he finally found reverse. The other two jumped in, and the Dodge vanished just as quickly as it had arrived.

Joseph watched as the taillights got smaller and smaller and finally disappeared in a cloud of dust. As Joseph watched the old Dodge through his field glasses, he could tell that it was definitely a sixty-four. He checked for a tag but the dust made it impossible for him to make out any numbers. He heard the truck backfire once more, and then silence overtook the compound. Joseph went over the details in his head. He knew there were three. He knew they drove an old and beat up vehicle they couldn't afford to repair so they probably had low income. And, most importantly, they now had the microchip.

After climbing back down from the spot where he had been watching, Joseph retrieved his faithful steed, Pegasus, and rode the cart back toward the outskirts of the city. He left the cart, and Pegasus, by the graveyard and thanked the donkey for its hard work. Joseph knew a cave system that led to the underground catacombs of the ancient ruins of the temple. It was a long walk, but it was covered, and fairly secretive. From there he walked through Zedekiah's Cave, a historic landmark for the Israelis and particularly important to the Masonic community. Each year the Freemasons of Israel held a ceremony in this cave. It was a ceremony of the Mark Master degree. Joseph's father, Ethan, had been the degree master for this ceremony, which had left Joseph lots of free time to explore the tunnels in the cave system, and he knew that it would open up again about a quarter-mile from the market district. Once again walking through the mammoth cavern, he felt safe for the first time in two days. The ceiling of the cave was almost eight meters high in places. There were giant limestone columns at various points, supporting the ceiling.

The echoes were amazing. A whisper could be spoken at one end of the cavern and be clearly heard at the other. It was like a giant auditorium. That was the particular reason that the Freemasons used it to hold their degrees. As Joseph had been taught during his initiation into the fraternity, his ancient brethren held their lodges on high hills, or in low dells. This was to serve as a safeguard against any possible "cowans," or eavesdroppers. Zedekiah's Cave was the perfect place to hold a degree ceremony. It was a sanctuary of enormous size. Still, the area could be safely cordoned off to ensure privacy.

Joseph had heard many stories about the caves during his childhood. Most of them were tales from his father. Ethan had explained to Joseph that the caves had been carved out by slaves and laborers over a period of many centuries. Ethan had also explained that the limestone was used as a building material primarily because it was so abundant, strong, and resistant to erosion. After his initiation as an Apprentice, Joseph learned that, according to legend, King Solomon, the first Grand Master, had used Zedekiah's Cave as the principle source of the material for Solomon's first temple. Being in such a place had fueled Joseph's interest and subsequent research on the subject. Searching for the temple had been more than a pastime; it brought him peace, as if the quest had been waiting for him to discover it.

As he continued to walk along the darkened limestone corridor he noticed his breath was becoming deeper and deeper, his footing becoming less sure with each step. He needed to get some rest.

The underground caves were cool and prone to a multitude of various rodents and other creatures, but the need for rest was too pressing to be overridden. It did not take Joseph long to find what he considered a suitable and safe place to bed down for the night. The clothing that he had borrowed from James was well made, and the garments provided Joseph with plenty of comfort from the dampness of the cave. Unable to fight it any longer, he curled up and closed his eyes.

Hunger almost prevented him from finding sleep, but eventually even that quieted into darkness and dreams. He dreamed of a small house downtown that he used to visit frequently, and of the food that had always waited for him, and of the hands that reached out in his sleep to hold him and wash his bleeding limbs. Then he was back in the hell that was the garbage dump, and around him, three figures bent, wrapped him in burlap, and tossed him into the bed of a truck.

6

As the compound faded into the night behind them, the three night stalkers began to breathe a little easier. The compound was out of sight, and their cargo was safe in the back of the truck. The day had been a nightmare of apprehension, believing that the overseer would be found. Now, as the truck lumbered down the road, spitting dust into the deep night, they could retreat to the countryside and dispose of the body, rid of it once and for all.

The cabin of the truck was dark and smelled of alcohol and the smoke that sputtered and puffed out the tailpipe. The dash lights had burned out years ago, and the only light was given by the intermittent blinking of the headlights as they flickered off and on with each bump. The men were forced to shift restlessly over the coils of the springs that punctured the seat; the one riding in the bed of the truck was just trying to hang on. He'd yelled out several times about slowing the vehicle down, trying to keep the body from bouncing into his lap with each swerve in the road, but had been ignored.

The passenger looked apprehensively onto the dark, unpaved roads passing under the tires. "Andrew, how much gas do we have—is there enough gas to get there?"

"Yes, dammit, I told you we have plenty of gas. Now will you please shut that slack mouth of yours?" There were no gas stations anywhere near where they were headed. The closest one was just outside the city, which was a good twenty-five or thirty kilometers away. The passenger almost jumped as the rider in the back banged against the glass. "Ignore him, he hasn't shut up since we started driving." Hazar nodded at his brother and cast his eyes back to the roadway. The knocking resumed and Andrew's hand whipped out, slamming the window with his fist, restoring silence for a minute or two. Hazar jumped again as a head poked itself in through his passenger side window.

"Hazar, Andrew, please. I have to stop, I need to piss. I'm begging you stop!" Andrew slammed on the brakes, and Hazar watched as their companion braced himself against the roof and side view mirror, almost launching into the roadway as the truck came to a halt. Getting down from the truck proved just a little too much. As he leapt from the bed, his left foot caught on the tailgate and he slammed, headfirst, into the roadway. Andrew burst into laughter.

As a smile cracked across Hazar's face, he rolled down his window calling out, "You are the epitome of grace, little brother!" Embarrassed, Paul got to his feet and walked down the road for about fifteen or twenty meters and stood on the edge without saying a word. Laughter was something he was used to.

After several minutes passed, the oldest brother, Andrew, called out. "Little brother, what is taking you so

long? I know it's small but it can't be that hard to find!"
Again the laughter.

Paul glanced down the roadway at the truck and smiled
despite himself. He had always been the butt of the joke.
Born small, Paul had tried to find ways to measure up to his
brothers, especially Andrew who had been built like a tank.
Taking a breath, Paul enjoyed another few minutes before
heading back to the truck—and the body. The first time
that his brothers had asked for his help, and this was where
he had been led. Shame welled up in the pit of his stomach
as he thought of what they had done, and tears formed in
the corners of his eyes.

It had been Paul who assaulted Joseph at the gate. He
thought he'd killed him when he clipped the overseer's
throat, then he'd panicked and run. But, he'd come back
with his brothers in the end, he'd stood with them, like a
man. He was twenty-two years old, but he had never lost
the softness of his childhood. For the first time he felt like
he had something in common with his brothers; in that
moment, he felt he had their respect. Quickly he wiped the
tears from his eyes and jogged back to where the truck sat
in the sole pool of light for miles.

He found his two brothers taking pulls off an old wine
bottle, and he could hear Andrew's voice as they quietly talked.
"How could I have done such a horrible deed to someone who
had been so good to me? A war hero! What was I thinking?
Why did I allow myself to be talked into such a scheme?"

"We need the money Andrew. It was a lot of money."
Hazar whispered, taking another drink from the bottle.

"Not enough," Andrew hissed back, his hands tight-
ening on the steering wheel. Hazar looked at his brother

for a moment, then glanced in his side mirror seeing Paul approaching.

"No, not nearly enough for what we have brought upon our family. But, it's done, right Paul?" Paul looked between his brothers before he nodded and scaled the tire back into the bed where he stared at the wrapped burlap. "We all did it. Paul you got him first, I . . . " Hazar shook himself as he remembered holding the metal L-shaped tool. The edge of the square had dug deep with each swing into the overseer's chest, and blood had soaked his shirt, but he wouldn't speak! "I attacked him with the straight edge. And Andrew, you—"

"I killed him."

The brothers were silent for a moment. Finally, Andrew turned the key, but silence remained, filling the cabin. Andrew wearily looked at Hazar, who reached beneath his seat and jiggled the battery connection.

Paul appeared at the window, "Why didn't he just tell us where they were? I just can't understand—we didn't need to kill him. I didn't want to kill him." Andrew cranked the key hard, and the car backfired as it started up, the shot echoing out into the emptiness of the night.

"Who knows, maybe he couldn't understand us in our English. It worked though; he didn't recognize our voices, but maybe he couldn't understand us at all. It's done now. Whatever the case, we have to see it through." Through a clenched jaw Andrew looked to each of his brothers who nodded and sat back as the truck lurched on again into the dark, dust flying out under the tires. "Hazar, look for a sign toward Budrus. That's where we need to turn."

Andrew knew that he had failed his brother. He was supposed to protect them, just as his mother had always done—always putting them before herself. He thought of how she would not agree to marry the man who would eventually become his stepfather until he could convince her that he would love her boys just as much as he loved his own. Andrew thought about how, after all of these years, his mother was going to have to hear how he, Hazar, and Paul had been involved in a murder. They had been driving for about an hour before Hazar pointed out the turn.

Having explored the mountains and outskirts of Budrus for many years when he was a boy, Andrew knew exactly where they would bury the body. Andrew took a small side road near the sign, barely visible on the curve, and almost indistinguishable from the brush around it. This created what Andrew called the "hidden passage." As they rounded another curve, Hazar could see a field that opened up on the right side and turned into a meadow. The field and meadow gradually ascended up toward the brow of a small hill where they pulled in.

Hazar pulled the lantern from under his seat and handed it to Paul as the three met up around the back of the truck. Hoisting the canvas-wrapped corpse between them, Andrew and Hazar each grabbed a small shovel from the truck bed. The lantern light cast long animated shadows across the field as they started to climb toward the brow of the hill.

The stars flickered and shone, the night almost moonless, as the three brothers lay down to catch their breath. Across Hazar, Andrew could hear Paul whispering under his breath, and for a moment felt anger rise in his chest before he let it subside. *Let the boy pray.* They all had faith at one point or another. Rising, Andrew drew the outline of a grave with the point of his shovel, and they started digging.

Climbing from the hole, Andrew looked over the work they'd completed. The earth was hard and filled with rocks, and thirty minutes of digging had only put them halfway. Pulling a flashlight from his pocket, Andrew disappeared downhill while Paul and Hazar kept shoveling up the begrudging earth. Walking several hundred meters along a small foot path, he made his way through the underbrush. He'd been ten years old when he first discovered this place. As a child, he'd spent hours upon hours pretending to fight prehistoric giants, slaying dragons, and saving one princess after another from his enemies. He'd hollowed out an acacia plant, carefully chopping away limbs, pruning back the inch long needles that covered each branch, and made a fortress for himself. That was his *sanctum sanctorum*. This was the place where he could escape from the reality of his poverty-stricken village, as well as the expectations of his family and brothers. There it stood before him: a wall of brush and overgrown needles. His sanctum had grown in on itself, and the safety of that shell had been lost as the plant grew and blossomed.

Pulling a large knife from his waistband, Andrew kneeled down in front of one of the small Acacia bushes near its larger mother plant. He dug around the bush with the knife until it loosened enough earth to where he could pull the roots from the ground. Even in his care to watch his hands, the needles drew blood to his curses as he headed back toward the hill and his brothers. They had made little progress.

"What is taking you two so long? You dig like a couple of girls!"

Hazar pulled a flask from his side, took a pull, and offered it to Paul who waved his hand. "We are little women for sure, so why doesn't our big sister hop down here with us and show us how to dig!"

Andrew jumped into the hole and in one move rose in a punch that left Hazar off balance and nursing a numb arm. Taking short breaks, they continued into the early morning hours. As the sun crested the horizon, the three stood around the grave, staring into the earth, the wrapped canvas lying beside it. Paul looked at his brothers.

"Should we say something?"

"If it makes you feel better that you've killed a man, go ahead." Hazar didn't lift his eyes as he looked into the pit. Paul was quiet, and with a nod to no one in particular Andrew placed a foot on the canvas and rolled the corpse into the hole. As the body hit the bottom, the sound was softer than the weight of a man's life should have made.

It only took them a fraction of the time to refill the grave, and Andrew dug a small hole at the head of the grave where he planted the sprig of acacia.

"I want to remember where the grave is located in case we need to move it." The others said nothing as he patted down the earth.

They all piled back into the truck. It started without incident, and they began back down the road to Budrus. They left the truck a few blocks away, covered by a tarp, before heading back to their small apartment. In a few days they would have the money they were promised, and in a few years, maybe they could forget the whole thing.

7

As the morning prayers rang out from the public service speaker, they reverberated through the cave system. Miraculously, Joseph found that he'd slept through the night. But, the awakening warned him that his cuts and muscles needed reprieve soon. It was Saturday, two nights since his attack, and the aroma of fresh-baked rolls from the market place told him that salvation might soon be at hand.

He needed to get to King George Street. As he walked along the back alleys and side streets of the city, he was careful not to draw attention to himself. He stopped at one of the storefront windows to check his reflection in the window glass. Luckily, the clothing he was wearing allowed him to blend in. As Joseph made it onto King George Street, he stopped in front of a small brown stucco shop in the Jewish Quarter. There was a single six-pointed star just over the doorway and a sagging clothesline leading across the alley to the other side. As he looked up the street, Joseph could see dozens of clotheslines going from one home to the next. By noon there would be freshly washed garments and towels stretched out on every one of them. He didn't realize how much he needed to see the city, just see life going on around him. Simple, everyday laundry and shopping reminded him that he wasn't as alone as he had felt since the attack.

Joseph knocked on the door several times before it was opened. "Shalom," he said softly. "How are you Mrs. Douglas?" It was Rachel's mother, Devorah. She gave him a startled look, but smiled and quickly ushered him inside. As Joseph walked in she quickly closed the door behind him.

Devorah reached up and gave Joseph a hug around his neck and kissed him on each cheek. "Joseph, why do you insist on putting me in your fairy tales?" she asked.

Joseph had known Devorah for as long as he could remember. "Please forgive me, old habits are hard to break."

"Well," she admonished, "You and Rachel need to start breaking some of those old habits."

As the widow mentioned Rachel, Joseph looked around. "Is Rachel here?"

"No, I sent her down to the market for some fresh strawberries. She will be back in just a few minutes."

"Surely, you aren't really upset that I called you the Widow Douglas?" Then he gave her another kiss on the cheek. The widow's face turned a little red, and she quickly changed the subject. Joseph remembered that even when Devorah was upset, she always managed to stay focused and concentrate on what was important. As Joseph thought back on those days he could not remember a single time— not once, not even for an instant—when he had ever known the widow to be unkind.

As Joseph hung the deceased young man's coat on a wooden peg behind the door, he could see the widow staring at the little dots of blood that had seeped into his shirt. To her credit, she acted as if she had not seen, asking instead, "So, what's with those tight clothes you're wearing?" He tried to act as if he hadn't heard. Smelling fresh bread from the kitchen, he walked past the living quarters into the kitchen. A half dozen or more freshly baked rolls and a couple of loaves of bread sat cooling on the counter. The two loaves of bread were freshly baked, still warm, and golden brown. His stomach gurgled at the aroma, and all his problems paled in comparison to the gnawing hunger in his belly. "What would a man have to do to get a couple of slices of bread?"

The widow looked at him, grabbed her bread knife from the kitchen drawer, and scolded, "It would be nice if a certain young man would just come around and visit a little more often—then he might not have to ask such foolish questions."

The widow pulled out a chair from the table and commanded Joseph to sit down. He did. He supervised hundreds of workers, he was a major project manager, he was personally responsible for the completion of the new temple, and he could usually get an audience with the king any time he wanted; yet, in this house, he had just been scolded and ordered to sit down like a child. Joseph watched the widow as she prepared the bread into French toast and boiled a pot of water for tea.

Joseph tried to control his salivation as the bread was sliced and soaked in a sweet mixture of milk, honey, eggs, cinnamon, and nutmeg, and each slice placed in a large sauté pan until the slices cooked to a golden brown. By the time she finished, Joseph had eaten four slices; each topped with maple syrup and a pinch of powdered sugar. He drank two or three cups of mint tea. All the while the widow chatted about the bakery and questioned him about the temple and Saul. Only her eyes betrayed her growing concern at the blood.

Finally she was unable to contain it. "Now that you're full and have taken my hospitality, tell me how you were hurt. Judging by the way you walked in here, your face isn't the only thing that could use some mending." As Joseph removed his shirt, the widow gasped.

Wordlessly she boiled some more water, washed and cleansed his wounds with a soft terry cloth, and dabbed some mercurochrome on his cuts. She wrapped his chest in gauze and clean white linen bandages. Joseph could see the tears that sparkled in her eyes. She was silent now, and Joseph was thankful towards her. *Thank you Devorah, for not prying into what I'm not yet sure I can reveal.* He needed to talk to Saul. With the skill of a surgeon, she finished and looked him over. "You need to get some rest."

"I'm not sure I have the time to do that just yet." Rising, Joseph kissed her cheek and thanked her for the wonderful breakfast. Promising he would visit again soon, he slung his coat back around him and walked out the door, back onto the bright streets of Israel, or at least he tried to.

As he was going out the door Joseph bumped right into Rachel as she was coming in. The smell of lilacs filled his senses as he looked down at her. Brown eyes ringed by thick lashes looked back up at him. Rachel's shoulder-length black hair bounced back slightly as she steadied herself.

"Rachel." There were moments when he wished he were better with words, and with Rachel looking into his eyes, this was one of those moments. He couldn't get over how great she looked.

"Joseph, I . . . how are you?" she asked.

Glancing at Rachel's mother he replied, "I'm fine. I mean, I've been better. It's really·great seeing you. You still look incredible."

"If you really think so, you should stop by more often. You know you're still my guy! What's with the suit?"

"That—" Joseph looked himself over and back at Devorah, "is something for later. I actually just stopped by, and I need to get moving." Moving around past her, Joseph managed to get himself onto the street.

"Can you stop by later, maybe for a cup of coffee?" Rachel stood in the doorway, half in and half out of the shop.

"I'll give it a try—coffee sounds great." Pausing for just a moment, Joseph gave Rachel a peck on the cheek. "I'll definitely be back for that coffee."

As Joseph faded from sight, the widow asked Rachel, "Did you notice that Joseph seemed a little more affectionate than usual?"

"Mamma, remember what you used to tell me? You used to say that a lady doesn't kiss and tell."

Rachel's mother laughed and said, "So, you have been listening to your mother."

8

Turning the corner from King George Street, Joseph headed down Schatz Street in the direction of the mall. The streets were lined with merchant stalls, and the walkway was just tight enough for two or three people to get through. Joseph could already feel himself sweating in the humidity as he spotted the palace guard. Just then he looked across the street and noticed one of them walking directly toward him. As he approached, Joseph was surprised to realize he recognized the man. Zabud was a brother in the Masons. Still trying to remain low profile, Joseph made his way to the guard and clasped the man's hand.

"Zabud, you have no idea how glad I am to see you."

Zabud squinted against the sun. "Joseph? Joseph! I thought maybe I was seeing things; I have been looking for you! Come quickly before someone else notices you." Zabud looked around the mall to see if anyone was watching, then he took Joseph by the right arm and escorted him off the street. They had not walked far when they entered a small shop.

Pushing past racks of men's clothing, Zabud walked Joseph toward the back and ushered him into what looked like a small changing room. As they entered, there was another door to the side which, to Joseph's surprise, opened to a winding spiral staircase that descended below the street. As they reached the bottom step, Joseph discovered that they were in one of the long underground corridors that ran throughout the city.

A series of underground passages had connected the city population to the original temple. Now, they were simply used as shortcuts to various parts of the palace. "Saul feared you were in danger, he commanded me and few other trustees to find you." Along the corridor, torches that were alternately hung every ten meters lit the way. Zabud and Joseph had walked about two or three hundred meters when they approached a second flight of ascending stairs. As they reached the top, Joseph found that they were standing at the outer door to what had once been one of the former king's special chambers. "This is as far as I go. Give the king my regards." As Zabud was about to leave, he clasped Joseph's hand and whispered into Joseph's ear. Watching Zabud disappear back down the corridor, Joseph turned and pushed through the door, and into the company of an old friend.

Sheikh Saleh Ben-Hadad turned toward him, his hand tugging at a thick beard. Joseph had not seen the sheikh in almost a year, and it was the sheikh, along with King Oman, that Joseph was scheduled to meet with the evening he was abducted, beaten, and left for dead. The sheikh, surprised at the sudden appearance, regained his composure as he realized who had come in behind him. The sheikh's smile unfolded.

"Joseph, how good to see you are all right. When you did not show two evenings ago, we feared the worst. It is good to see you so well."

"And you, Achi," replied Joseph.

After a little small talk, the sheikh told Joseph that he was aware that something must have happened. "You are always so prompt and dependable, Joseph. Are you sure everything is all right? Was there any problem with the temple that I might help you with?"

Joseph stopped and apologized for his absence the previous evening.

The sheikh was studying him. "You look tired. Why don't you freshen up and get some rest."

Joseph was sure it was true. Even the widow's breakfast could not replace a night's sleep in a real bed. "I think I will. Thank you for the suggestion." As their brief encounter came to an end, the sheikh bid Joseph a good day, parting with, "Shalom."

Joseph turned toward the sheikh and extended his hand, but the man shied away, guarding a wrist. "I must apologize, I hurt my hand while playing with my grandson; you know how rough little ones can be." Joseph nodded and replied, "I do—take care of that hand."

As the sheikh turned and exited, the door at the end of the antechamber opened.

"Good morning, sir." The man was one of King Oman's personal assistants. "The king will be with you in a moment. I apologize for the wait but I was only made aware of your appearance a moment ago. I am Phillip. Please let me know if there is anything that I can help you with."

Joseph nodded. "Thank you, actually I was just talking with an old friend."

"Yes? I didn't catch who it was, only heard your voices through the door. May I ask if Zabud encountered any trouble getting you to the palace?"

Joseph tried to hide his surprise. "No, no trouble, in fact it was a turn of fate that I wound up right where Sheikh Saleh Ben-Hadad had been waiting," he said, finding a seat at a small table in the corner. Joseph felt his muscles unwind into the cushion.

Philip's eyes were questioning, "The sheikh? I wasn't aware he was scheduled to meet the king today."

Joseph glanced toward the closed door from where the sheikh had exited. "Perhaps he had a private audience?"

"Possibly, though it was probably a schedule mix up. Anyway, I'm glad to hear there was no incident. I asked about Zabud because we have had some problems with beggars in the tunnels as of late; the king has been, perhaps, too lenient with their presence." Joseph remembered that the king always had a soft place in his heart for the underprivileged in the city.

Changing the conversation, Joseph told Phillip, "The last couple of times that I visited with the king, I got to know Samuel pretty well. Is he around?"

Phillip advised that Samuel was running errands for the king. "Can I have him summoned for you? We could send a runner perhaps."

"No, no, that's OK. I just wanted to say hello, ask him about his art." Except for the fact that he was clean shaven, Phillip reminded Joseph of the deceased young man, James.

"Sir, you have done a nice job on the new project at the compound," remarked Phillip.

"Thank you Phillip, but it wasn't me. The king has final approval on all the plans."

"You are too modest, sir. From what I have heard you have his complete trust and permission with the project." After a pause he continued, "He has also told me many stories . . . about your adventures. He has encouraged me to call you—Little John."

Joseph had to laugh as the memory of a less complicated time rushed through his head. The king had been, and still was, his very best friend—the best friend that Joseph had ever had. It made Joseph feel good to know that the king still remembered the adventures of their youth.

"Did I not say it correctly, sir?"

"Yes, you said it exactly right, Phillip." Joseph decided that if the king had told Phillip about their childhood, and had mentioned those escapades they shared in their youth, then Saul must also consider Phillip a very trusted friend. For the first time, Joseph noticed that he had been sitting at the king's Chess table, the set sitting on a beautiful ornate mahogany stand.

"Do you know the game, sir—chess?"

Joseph smiled, "Yes, the king and I used to play many years ago, before we became preoccupied with more complicated things."

"If I might ask, what is your favorite piece?"

Joseph looked up at Phillip, "My favorite piece . . ."

"Yes sir, I have found that a lot can be inferred from the selection. Each piece has its own place, function, and difficulty, if you'll pardon me for prying."

As Joseph looked up, he noticed the king standing just inside the doorway. Without missing a beat, Joseph looked directly at the king and plucked the lead figure off the board. "Why, it's the king of course."

With a laugh the king continued on into the room. "Don't let him fool you Phillip. He knows that the king is the weakest piece on the board. That is why he is always surrounded by the other more flexible and versatile pieces."

Joseph gave a small bow. "Who am I to disagree with King Oman?"

Saul turned to Phillip. "Could you give Joseph and me a few minutes?" With a nod, Phillip left the room, closing the door behind him. "I have been worried about you, my brother," the king said.

"I have done a little worrying myself, Your Majesty," Joseph replied.

"Joseph, please, you don't have to be so formal."

With a deep bow, Joseph replied, "Yes, Your Majesty."

The king just shook his head. "What am I going to do with you?"

"Well I would ask you to raise me from the dead, but I managed to do that already once since you've seen me."

The king's eyebrows raised as he looked over the cuts and bruising still apparent on Joseph's face. "I can do many things, Achi, but I'm not sure I know that particular trick."

"Neither did I, and I had to learn it quickly, but would you mind waiting until I could have a shower and perhaps a change of clothes? These last few nights have been—" Joseph noticed the king's eyes darting over him, noting the tight clothes, the bags under his eyes, and the dust that coated his bedraggled hair, ". . . difficult," he finished.

"This," the king said, pulling a cell phone out of his pocket, "is a trick I know. Phillip? See to it that Joseph has an opportunity to take a shower and get him a set of fresh clothes from my personal closet." The king dangled the phone between his fingers. "This thing has replaced two secretaries and all the hand bells of the palace."

"Things were much simpler when we were younger, wouldn't you agree, Your Majesty?" asked Joseph, again slumping into the chess table's soft chair.

"You mean when you and I were rescuing Becky Thatcher from the villainous forces of Injun Joe, or the fair maiden from the sheriff of Nottingham?" replied the king.

"Something like that," Joseph laughed.

"By the way, how are Rachel and her mother?"

Joseph's brow furrowed. "I didn't even know anyone had seen me this morning." A short rap at the door interrupted his next question. As Phillip reappeared, the paper tucked neatly under one arm, he announced that the shower was ready.

It was just like when they were children—there was nothing that escaped Saul's knowledge. "They are well, Your Majesty. I saw them just this morning. The widow and I had breakfast."

Throwing his hands up in a gesture of appeasement, the king said, "I apologize if you felt I was snooping, I do keep an eye on my closest friends, but I can assure you that this time, the report on you was entirely without my orders." Laughing, the king watched Joseph's face contort in confusion. "That may have made it sound even more sinister. I promise you, Achi, there is nothing strange here, but I don't feel I should be the one . . . " The king stopped himself, shaking his head and waving Joseph off. "Just go, Achi, before you make me trip over my own tongue."

Sighing—and thus emitting more chuckles from the king—Joseph turned to leave with Phillip, but he stopped at the door. "Oh, one more thing—it's probably nothing, but earlier I met Sheikh Ben-Hadad outside your study."

"Yes, I was aware he was on the premises. He was probably confused when he was supposed to be meeting with me. The sheikh was probably just embarrassed. He's getting old you know."

With a short bow, Joseph followed Phillip out of the room and down a series of hallways. Without a guide it would be a simple feat to become lost within the palace, but the familiar halls of his childhood yielded easily to him, and nostalgia played at the edge of his thoughts. Unfortunately, nothing was quite familiar enough to trigger a memory. Besides, there were many less majestic places in which to get lost. Joseph had gone over the blueprints a hundred times when he had been working on extensions to the palace, and being in its halls felt almost like second skin. Finally they came to a door, and Phillip's crisp steps came to a halt as, in one smooth movement, he opened the door and stepped aside for Joseph to enter. "Just give me a call on the intercom if there is anything you need."

As he heard the door click closed behind him, Joseph was left to take in the beauty of what he recognized as the king's personal spa. The entryway was lined with beautiful rich cedar panels, and the door was heavy with natural color. Passing through a small alcove, the room opened up into the main bathing room. A small table supported a vase with fresh flowers, and decorative lamps lit the room and the magnificent-looking statue that was the centerpiece. Even in his fatigued state the grandeur was intoxicating, and Joseph felt himself drawn to it. The statue depicted a beautiful young woman standing over a broken column. Before her was an open book, and in her right hand she held what Joseph recognized to be a sprig of acacia; in her left hand was an urn. Behind her, the unmistakable figure of Father Time was unfolding and counting the ringlets of the young woman's hair. The sculpture was surrounded by a backdrop of crystal-cut glass and mirrors that gave an infinite illusion of the sculpture continuing through the wall.

As *infinite as time itself,* Joseph mused as he undressed. Next to the statue on the adjoining wall hung a gold-framed oil painting of two women drawing water from an ancient well. To Joseph's amazement, he realized that the painting wasn't a print. It was signed in the bottom right hand corner with the initials E.D. Stepping back, Joseph took in the painting anew and made a mental note to ask Phillip who the artist was. The floor was polished black marble with intricate gold inlayed designs in each of the squared tiles. There were smaller inlayed squares at each point of the larger ones creating a three-dimensional effect that played tricks on the eyes, almost causing him to lose his balance.

Managing to regain his focus, he walked under two archways that led him into the shower area. Between the two archways, in the center of the floor, was another familiar and very old symbol that he had come across before. Inlaid in the floor and encircling the symbol was a gold inscription. It was written in Latin. Joseph recognized the inscription: *beatus homo qui invenit sapientiam.* As he walked around the symbol Joseph read the text out loud, "Blessed is the man who finds wisdom." Joseph couldn't remember if the text was from Proverbs or not. He decided that he would look it up at his first opportunity.

The king's bathroom contained more fine art than any home that Joseph had ever been to, but even that might have been dwarfed in cost to the shower itself. It was huge. Four gold showerheads protruded from each direction on different levels, two installed just above head height, and two at the waist. Inlayed within the walls above the showerheads were large flat screen TVs—three of them—and they were all turned on. All three of the TVs were on the same channel and it appeared to be a re-broadcast of a show originating from the United States. Joseph's English was actually pretty good, and he was able to follow *Good Morning America* as he showered, the hot water relieving muscles that he had taxed to the limit.

There was no sound, but the captions unrolled at the bottom of the screen. They were talking about *Slumdog Millionaire*, the big winner of the Academy Awards. Pictures of the ghettos of Mumbai flashed across the screen as the commentators talked about the living conditions and squalor. Joseph remembered traveling with the king to Mumbai when he officially started working for him back in 1995. The conference had been black-tie, but the king had requested that Joseph accompany him. They'd flown directly into the Chattrapathi Shivaji International Airport and stayed in the royal suite at the Renaissance Convention Centre for three full days. Comen Yusef had even been playing, and after the show the king had arranged a meeting with the legendary musician. The honor kept growing with the king being awarded the Order of the Knight of York.

The York Rite Masonic degree is based on events from the time of King Athelstan, who reigned as king of England from 924 to 939.

King Athelstan was the son of Edward the Elder and grandson of Alfred the Great. The significance of the degree is its association with the five points of fellowship and their relationship and correspondence with the five petals of a rose. As Joseph continued to watch the camera pan across the collapsing houses and grime of the slums, he noticed that his fingers had become wrinkled and saturated by the water, and the steam was making it increasingly hard to breathe. He stepped out of the water and found that a towel had been left for him to dry off. In the front alcove, clothes had been laid out, along with a pair of Berluti shoes; everything was in Joseph's size. Next to the clothes, a roll of bandages and gauze had been arranged for him. The king must have noticed as much as Devorah.

As he finished dressing his wounds and getting dressed, Joseph watched as the pictures on the TV changed to show several beautiful Mumbai Indian dancers, each dancer dressed in matching gold and red outfits. But Joseph's mind had already wandered back to his three assailants, and where they had buried James's body. The old Dodge truck they had been driving might lend a clue to who they were. Hopefully, with the king's resources, he might be able to track it down. Joseph knew that with almost a half-million people in the city, there were probably many old trucks still in use, especially in the suburban areas. Still, it had the rusted top and hood and the passenger door that was off-color. An old truck viewed at a distance in the middle of night wouldn't play well with police, but maybe it could be located. As Joseph finished getting dressed, he made his way from the shower back to the area adjacent to the king's private chambers. Phillip entered just after him with a tray of fresh fruit and refreshments.

"Was your shower suitable? Can I offer you a cup of mint tea, Little John?"

Smiling, Joseph took the tea. "Do you know who the artist was that painted the portrait next to the spa entrance? It was called *Two Women at the Well*? I didn't recognize the initials, E.D."

"I'm sorry, I'm afraid I'm not particularly known for my taste in art; the king hired me for other reasons."

"Other reasons?" Joseph looked the man over. "And what might those be beyond making a wonderful cup of tea."

Philip paused and looked quizzically at Joseph. "You mean you couldn't tell, sir? Why, he hired me as a combat specialist." For a moment the two just stared at each other before Phillip broke into a grin and Joseph broke into laughter. "Well, His Majesty hired me for my humor. Anyway, is there anything else I might get you, sir?"

"Actually yes, a paper bag would be useful—I need to return some clothes to a friend." Joseph thought about the empty coffin and the toll his actions could take on the unknowing family.

"A paper bag, sir?" Phillip asked. "I will be happy to bag up your old clothes for you, if that is what you wish, and I will find out who the artist is. In fact, if you run into Samuel, you have as good a chance as I to ask him. He *is* our art specialist. He was employed by the king as an artist to paint various frescoes at the palace and in the new temple." As he finished, Phillip placed a second cup of tea next to

Joseph's and returned to the cart. Just as he gripped the cart's handle, the king entered from a side door.

"I hope my tea is still hot, Phillip." Phillip gave Joseph a wink out of the corner of his eye, turned, and advised the king that he was going to attend to the gentleman in the library. Then he left the room.

"Joseph,"—the king's look penetrated him—"you've been hurt. I was bewildered when you failed to show at the meeting you scheduled with the sheikh and me. That's not who you are. I sent several men I trust to check for you, as did Ben-Hadad. The sheikh's men reported no car at the compound or at your home. I had the police search for it, and they found it near the port, burned and abandoned. I set up men to find you, but luckily you ran into Zabud. Now, what the hell happened? Your nose looks nearly broken, and I can tell by your wincing that the injuries beneath your shirt must be far worse than that."

Joseph blurted, "I am sorry, Your Majesty. I feel that this is the start of another attempt on your life." Silence filled the room, only broken by the soft *clink* as the king placed his teacup back into its saucer.

"Slow down, Joseph; it is your life that I have feared for," replied the king, his eyes falling to his hands, resting on either side of his porcelain cup. He then asked Joseph, "Where did it happen?"

"At the compound, they took my car and left me in the garbage. From what I could tell, there were only three of them." Saul listened carefully as Joseph related the attack and his desperate trek back to town.

"So, what you're saying is that they know their way around the compound as well as you do?" Joseph opened his mouth and quickly closed it, not wanting to think about the implications. "It is my nature to be suspicious, and my job as well. You would not speak against your workers—I know you trust them as fellow Masons—but you are saying that these thugs knew their way around the property as well as you did?"

"Yes, Your Majesty," Joseph looked into Saul's eyes and cursed his stupidity for not seeing it sooner, "you are right."

Slowly the king sipped from his tea before continuing, "It could have been a mugging—one you were lucky to survive—praise be to Him. Those clothes were not your own, so they took those, along with your cell phone as you didn't call for help. They also took your watch."

Joseph grabbed his left wrist and lowered his eyes, "I am sorry, Achi; I treasured that watch."

"When you picked up the chess piece I noticed the pasty shadow it left on your wrist." The king picked up Joseph's wrist between his thumb and forefinger and dangled it until Joseph snatched it away.

"The phone I'm not sure of—it was lost in the struggle—but this was not just thieves, Saul. They asked me . . ." Joseph found Saul's eyes. "They asked me, 'What is more important, my king or my life.' They kept demanding something from me, yelling at me for my soul. I still don't understand any of it."

Joseph's muscles had gone rigid as he remembered their screaming faces, and he felt Saul's hand on his shoulder. "Are you OK, Achi?"

Joseph nodded and took a deep breath to calm his nerves. "I just really haven't given myself too much time to think about it."

"So, that is why you were at the widow's this morning. She is a good woman."

"She cleaned my wounds and fed me. I think that without her, and seeing Rachel, I wouldn't have had the strength to make it to Zabud."

Saul smiled. "The smell of lilacs has always given you strength, my friend. And, I believe you that this is more than a mugging. For a few weeks, I have been hearing whispers. I think—" The king sighed and finished his tea in one gulp, "I think that they were trying to get you to defect, and did a poor job of it. I think, they wanted your 'soul' cooperation. Our friendship has not gone unnoticed by my enemies." Saul's eyes held pain as he looked at Joseph. "I am sorry you have been pulled into this, Achi."

"I have more, Your Majesty. The men who assaulted me also have my necklace, that which you gave as a *gift*." The king sat back in his chair in confusion, his mouth falling open and his eyes widening.

"The necklace—it was stolen?" Joseph nodded and continued to relate his luck at the grave. Saul's expression slowly changed from a look of surprise to a smile as Joseph told the king about the transmitter.

"Get me the transmitter frequency, and I'll give you one of my cars. We need to move on this quickly. I'll see what I can get on that truck's description."

"Thank you, Your Majesty, but I'm OK without taking one of your cars," answered Joseph.

"A car is a car Joseph; it is replaceable, just like the watch. Do you know what the name Rolex means?" Joseph shook his head. "Nothing! The name Rolex was chosen simply because it was clear, easy to spell, and easy to pronounce in many languages. It was meant to be easy and so it is easy to lose. But, there are some things that are more than what they appear. I'm glad we will recover the necklace, as small as it is; it meant a lot to us when we were children, and perhaps more to me now."

They were silent for a moment as each digested and considered the repercussions of the events. Standing, Saul looked at Joseph. "What do you think they were after, Achi? 'Give us your soul?'"

"I don't know, Your Majesty. If they wanted my cooperation, killing me wouldn't gain it."

"Are you sure that is what they were saying, Joseph? *Soul?*" The king shook his head. "Perhaps they were saying my name? Give us Saul?"

"Your Majesty, Saul, I have been having thoughts ever since I got attacked at the compound."

"What kind of thoughts?" asked the king.

"Memories, I think, ones from before I was injured." Saul sat back down in his chair, examining Joseph as he continued, "And, dreams of when I was just a boy. It's just flickers, but I remember you, I think, and Rachel, and something we found in a cave. I know they said I may never remember, but it didn't feel like a dream." Joseph's eyes were searching as he looked again at Saul. "Does any of this sound familiar?"

Saul's lips were tight on his face as he thought. "The doctors have told me not to rush you. They told me that it could cause a relapse. We . . . we had many adventures in the caves when we were young—Tom and Huck, Robin and Little John, Jachin and Boaz."

Joseph looked at him. "The two pillars of King Solomon's temple in the book of Kings?"

Saul looked at his friend through furrowed eyes. "You were always obsessed with the first temple; you pestered me and my father for answers constantly, researching. I can't count the number of times you thought you knew *exactly* where it was located. But when you had your accident you just—stopped talking about them, and about the caves. Go slowly my friend, the past holds pitfalls as much as it holds treasure."

Joseph took his time going back over the details while explaining to the king how he had come to put the body of the deceased young man in his place. He slowly explained his plans for recovery. All the while, Saul paced the room, his chin tucked into his chest, grunting approval or shaking his head.

"Joseph, I think that you may have done more than just recover your necklace, *if* we play our cards right. I'll have to make a few calls, but, yes, I think this may play out quite nicely. With a little luck we can flush out the men who attacked you. While you were in the shower, I contacted a friend at the Central Police District and asked him to stop by for a visit. He might keep us informed about any suspicious activity the police notice. I also thought we might put in a report of the watch, in case anyone tried to sell it. The police will disseminate the information to pawners. He's only an inspector, but his clout goes a lot further than that." As they walked, Saul stopped just outside the main door to the library. "Do not worry, Joseph. You can speak freely to the inspector. I have known him for many years, and I trust him. You may know him as well, from years ago. He is a good man."

The king's words were reassuring, if confusing. Joseph had not seen the royal library in many years, and as the door slid open, the massive collection took him by surprise. Thousands of books covered every wall, from the floor to the ceiling; and dark, wooden running ladders lined each corner. "Inspector?" inquired the king. "Inspector, where are you?"

From the second floor of the library a husky voice responded, "I'm up here, Your Majesty. I'm on my way." Joseph watched as the inspector appeared at the railing on the second floor directly above and behind them. "I am sorry, Your Majesty; you know I always try to capitalize whenever I visit. Books! I love books." The inspector continued to talk as he made his way to one of the four winding staircases that were at each corner of the library. "Isn't this place magnificent? The smell even! I'm just like a kid in a candy store each time I get through these doors." As the inspector finally made his way down the stairs, the king met him and introduced Inspector Ben-Zur to Joseph.

"It's a pleasure to meet you, inspector." The inspector looked at Joseph and then at the king, perplexed.

"You don't remember me do you, Joseph?"

Clearing his throat, Saul interrupted, "Joseph served our military with distinction and suffered an affliction during his service."

Joseph laughed and interrupted, "What the king means to say is that my memory is not what it once *was*.

I'm sorry, Inspector. Did I cause you problems when I was a mischievous boy running through the streets?"

The king intervened, "Joseph, I think maybe that you know the inspector from another time. Inspector Ben-Zur was the lead investigator when your father was . . ."

"Oh," Joseph looked at the man's grizzled beard and well-kept suit. "Oh! I'm sorry I . . . Inspector, I am sorry I didn't recognize you."

"Please, call me David," replied the inspector, with a soft smile. As they each shook the other's hand they both recognized the customary handshake and grip that was used by lodge brothers all over the world. The inspector was a man of average height and looked to weigh between ninety-five and a hundred kilos. His dark curly hair was slightly graying and receding at the temples. He had heavy arched brows, and thick reading glasses provided a half shield below his green eyes. His khakis and cashmere pullover gave the impression that he was a man who dressed with comfort in mind.

"How long have you been with the force now, Inspector?"

Ben-Zur's brow furrowed. "Joseph, really, just call me David. And, if I make it until October, I will have thirty-seven years in with the bureau." Joseph's jaw must have dropped because Ben-Zur broke into laughter.

"Thirty-seven years? Shouldn't you be a commander or bureau chief by now?" Joseph asked.

"Joseph," said the king, "the inspector has been honored with many commendations. And he has been offered promotions on five different occasions. However, he advised that he won't accept promotion until he finishes one of his unsolved cases."

"Very nicely put, Your Majesty, and thank you," replied the inspector.

"My father . . ." Joseph looked at the man, "You mean to tell me that after all of these years you're still working on my father's case?"

"The inspector and I have had many conversations pertaining to your father's case over the years, Joseph," replied the king.

"Have you developed any new leads?"

"Well, just let me say that I am always working," answered the inspector.

"Thank you. I know that my father would be pleased to know that he has not been forgotten," responded Joseph. "But, I don't think he would have wanted his death to limit the successes of such a good man."

"Joseph, I will never stop looking for the impious wretch who murdered your father," replied the inspector. "I'd rather be an inspector, and feel like I have fulfilled my obligation, than be a commissioner with a guilty conscience."

"Let us change gears just a bit, Inspector. I am sorry to have bothered you with something so trivial, but Joseph's watch was stolen, and finding it may have much larger repercussions."

"A watch? That might be hard to find—people grift and sell them all over the place. Monetarily speaking, how much are we talking about?"

"Clearly, it's not about the money, Inspector, but I would value it at around sixteen thousand mint, ten thousand after market. I know a uniformed officer could just have easily taken down the information, but we were afraid that it would just get lost in all of the paperwork, and we needed this handled with care." The inspector gave a slight smile of gratitude and told the king that he appreciated his concern and that he was right.

The king handed him a paper with the details of the watch. The inspector looked at the information written on the paper that the king had provided and started mumbling to himself.

"OK—let's see what you have here: one Rolex presidential watch—18 karat yellow gold crown, custom diamond lugs, custom blue diamond dial, eight round and two baguette-cut diamonds, scratch resistant crystal, with forty round-cut diamonds surrounding the bezel. It has an Italian-made gold bracelet with 312 smaller diamonds. Well, I guess we won't have to worry too much about serial numbers!"

"It is a very nice watch, Inspector," answered the king.

"Well, my young friend," the inspector turned, "how does someone lose a watch practically made of diamonds?" At a loss, Joseph looked to the king.

The inspector grinned. "I am only kidding. Like we discussed, I know how to use a subtle hand. I'll get started immediately. Granted, it will be like trying to find a needle in a haystack, but with any luck they will try to pawn it locally."

The king spoke up and said, "That is why I called you personally, I knew that you would take the time to run down every lead."

Knowing his love of food, the king also advised the inspector that he had taken the liberty of asking Phillip to bring in some fresh bagels, coffee, and tea. They would dine in the library conference room.

The inspector was all smiles. "Joseph, now you see why I enjoy coming around here so much." Phillip entered with the bagels, tea, and coffee. It was as if the man were everywhere in the palace.

"Stay as long as you want, Inspector, especially if you wish to get caught up on your reading." Ben-Zur got up from his seat, bowed to the king, and thanked him for his generous hospitality.

As they walked the halls back toward the king's chambers, Joseph asked, "Do you think the inspector will have any luck?"

"Probably not, but he is a good man, and it might be beneficial to have him a little familiar with what is about to happen. I wasn't lying about the influence that man has over the department." Suddenly the king stopped in the hall and grabbed Joseph's arm. "Joseph, I would like you to go away for a while. I'll have Phillip get you a new phone." Seeing that Joseph was about to object, the king silenced him. "Joseph, I am your king and you will obey me." His expression softened as he took hold of Joseph's hand in a recognized grip. "Things are going to start moving quickly around here, and I need you to lie low if we are to get to the bottom of this." Leaning forward, the king whispered into Joseph's ear and Joseph whispered into his. The king swept past him, and as they parted the king gave one last piece of cautioning advice, "Achi, be on the lookout for wolves in sheep's clothing. You know they are always at the door."

Joseph quickly navigated his way down the three flights of stairs from the king's study and found himself on the side street entrance. Phillip was there waiting for him.

"The king let me know that you were leaving. Here, sir, I have your package." A new cell phone was handed over but Phillip did not immediately release it when Joseph reached. Phillip's grip was surprisingly powerful as he looked into the man's eyes. "Don't lose it." Joseph acknowledged it as the king's request. In his other arm, Phillip held a small brown wrapped package. "It's that dead boy's clothes; I was able to identify the family by the time the funeral was held. Shall I hold off on returning them until we see how far our plans go?"

Joseph nodded and tucked the cell phone into his pocket. Saul had a plan, he could tell, and right now Joseph's part was to lie low. He shook Phillip's hand and made his way into the crowded streets.

10

The city was bustling with the activity of the shops, merchants, street vendors, tourists, and beggars that filled every corner. Each beggar had a personal story, or some trick that he hoped would earn him a shekel or two to put in his pocket. The current exchange rate was about four and a quarter shekels for each U.S. dollar. Usually the yanks were the easiest targets, offering quadruple the benefits in success. They could always be counted on to give a little something to the beggars. If nothing else they gave in just so they wouldn't have to be confronted. Joseph remembered being at this one beggar's corner once when he overheard an exchange with an American tourist. Thinking back on it, Joseph had laughed until he cried.

This tourist was walking down the street with his wife when the beggar appeared from a hidden doorway. Walking up to the man, the beggar asked if he was an "honest man." Naturally the tourist would answer that he was an honest man. Once the tourist answered, the beggar made his proposition. Looking down at the tourist's feet, the beggar told him that just from the look of them—without even reading the label—he could tell the man and his wife exactly where he had gotten his shoes. Moreover, if he could not accurately tell where he had gotten them, the beggar would clean and polish both pairs for free. If he could manage this amazing, borderline mystic feat, this show would be worth ten of the tourists' U.S. dollars. The tourist looked at his wife and knew that he was in way too deep to recant; so, the tourist advised the beggar that if he could tell him exactly where he had gotten his shoes, he would give him the ten dollars.

"Now, you said that you were an honest man," said the beggar one last time. "And you agree that if I can tell you where you got them shoes, you will give me ten U.S. dollars," asked the beggar.

"Yes, that is exactly right," said the tourist. With that, the beggar looked down at the shoes on the tourist's feet and said,

"Sir, you got them shoes right there on your feet."

And with that the tourist reared back and laughed, pulled his wallet out of his pocket, found a ten-dollar bill, and handed it to the beggar saying, "That's a lesson well learned." The beggar tipped his hat, thanked the man for being so honest and scooted down the street to attend to his next victim.

Continuing to walk along the streets, Joseph could tell that it was going to be another unusually warm day. In the distance he could see young Israeli children playing with toy guns, playing out conflicts with Palestinians and Hamas. In a few short years the guns in their hands would be real, and they would understand that there were better things to imagine. As he walked past, Joseph began to feel the prickly chill of being watched.

Rubbing down the hairs on the back of his neck, Joseph tried to glance out of the corners of his eyes. He had learned to heed his senses in the army, and they'd saved him more than once. Someone was following him. He stepped from the sidewalk and into the street, walking beside the vehicles parked along the street and checking the vehicles' side mirrors. At first he couldn't tell a thing; there were just too many people. He stopped in front of one of the local stores and checked the reflection in the window. Someone was watching him from across the street. A brimmed hat and glasses covered his face, but his attention was unmistakable. For a few feet, Joseph continued down the line of cars, pretending not to notice his shadow. The feeling on his neck was growing more intense, and he realized he'd lost track completely of the man.

Breaking into a light jog he made it to Schatz Street, the beginning of the heart of the city where the crowds grew thickest, where he ducked inside the Montefiore Hotel. The Montefiore was located where Jaffa and King George Street met Zion Square near the Great Synagogue. The hotel was also near the Ben Yehuda Pedestrian Mall; a side entrance connected the two for guest use. Quickly, Joseph entered the Montefiore and headed straight for the side entrance. Tourists crowded the hotel lobby.

Tourists were easy to spot. Most of them didn't know what to bring or how to dress. The hotel was exquisitely decorated with contemporary furnishings. Each guest room had all the modern amenities, including wireless Internet connections. The hotel's bar-lounge and coffee shop could satisfy the taste of any connoisseur. The pedestrian mall and the city's talented work force had been a welcome staple to the city's sluggish economy. However, in recent years and months, Joseph knew firsthand that it had become the favorite place of the suicide bomber. The bombers knew about the multitude of people at the pedestrian malls and took full advantage of selecting places where they felt they could do the most damage, making the biggest statements.

Hoping the mall would be just as crowded as usual, Joseph figured that he could get lost in the crowd, if the slip through the hotel hadn't already lost his tail. Joseph made his way along the mall, keeping to the shadows and trying to stay out of sight. He stopped several times and looked around. If someone was still following him, he was blending in perfectly.

"OK, where did you go?" Scanning the crowd, Joseph realized he was alone, and he slowly released the breath he hadn't been aware he was holding. *Had he imagined it?* Either way, now was not a time to err on care. Joseph stopped and waited a few minutes, just to be safe, before he continued down the mall. He realized that he was once again in familiar territory. King George's Street put him only about a block from Widow Douglas's home, and he *had* told Rachel he would be back for coffee. He walked down two more side streets and cut across the alleyway before he came to the door with the blade and chalice painted above it, and he knocked. The door opened slightly and Joseph could see Rachel standing just inside.

"I don't believe it, twice in one day? Mamma, come quick, it's a miracle!" As Joseph leaned in a little closer,

Rachel asked him, "Why are you sneaking around?" Joseph pushed open the door, quickly entered, and closed the door behind him. He looked out the window. "What are you doing? And who are you hiding from?"

Joseph turned toward Rachel, "I am not hiding. I just don't want to let any pests in."

Rachel folded her arms. "It looks like you're hiding. Besides, I just *let* the pest in."

"Rachel, leave him alone." Rachel's mother entered, rubbing her hands on a towel.

"Hello Mrs. Douglas," Joseph smiled, but he was greeted with a tight-lipped stare.

"Take off your shoes, wash your hands, and get ready for lunch—and my name is not Mrs. Douglas. To you my name is Devorah. And you are old enough now to know the difference."

As Joseph removed his shoes and placed them beside the door, he noticed that Rachel was watching him. "You've changed your clothes since this morning." She moved toward him, grabbed his shoulder, and pulled him toward her, mussing his hair and sniffing, "Mmmmm, somebody smells like they just came from a Turkish bath house."

"Rachel, stop that. How many times do I have to tell you to leave Joseph alone?"

Joseph quickly agreed, "Yeah Rachel, listen to your mother." Rachel just rolled her eyes, mumbled some comment about Joseph always being the favorite, and went into the kitchen. The widow and Joseph followed, and Joseph moved to the sink to wash his hands. He and Rachel sat down at the table as Rachel's mother finished setting the places. The widow had made a tortellini salad and had a Greek turkey sub on each plate. She also had Rachel set out a bottle of Dalton merlot, one of Joseph's favorite wines. It was a dark purple wine from the vineyards of the northern region. The wine was made from a mixture of plums, cherries, and homemade jam, all blended together and balanced by faint shades of vanilla that was extracted from the barrel as it was left to age. Uncorking the bottle, Joseph hovered his nose just above the lip and took in the bouquet.

"Mamma's been saving it just for you." Devorah's eyes quickly cut toward her. "Well it's *true*, Mamma." In an audible whisper she continued, "I was going to open a bottle of it a couple of weeks ago, but Mamma snatched it out of my hand and put it back into the pantry." Rachel's mother was quick to set the record straight.

"I was not saving the wine specifically for Joseph, or for anyone else. I just did not want Rachel wasting it on that good for nothing *shaygitz* she had brought home." As Rachel's mother finished making her comment, Joseph heard a knock on the backdoor. "Ah, Joseph, I hope you don't mind one more guest." Alarm bells sounded in his head—the widow and Rachel were one thing, they were people he could trust, but Saul had given him specific instructions. Who else was here? More importantly, were they persons who might ruin his attempt to keep a low profile?

Rising from his seat, and eyeing the distance back to the front door, Joseph apologized, "I was not aware that you were having other guests. I shouldn't crowd your table." Rachel grabbed Joseph's arm as he was rising and forcefully invited him to sit back down.

"Don't worry Joseph," she said. "It's just a friend who comes by to check on Mamma. I think you two know each other." As Joseph looked back toward the restroom, Samuel was standing in the doorway.

"*Bonjour Monsieur, comment allez-vous?*" inquired Samuel.

"Samuel, *pour quoi sont vous ici?*" Rachel's eyebrows rose as she took note of Joseph's fluency in French as he asked Samuel why he was there. Samuel just looked at Joseph, apologized to the mademoiselle for being late, and took a seat next to Rachel.

Rachel's mother took a seat by Joseph. "Could you two young men be kind enough to speak in a language that I can understand?"

Joseph looked at the widow. "I'm sorry. You're right. We were being rude. So tell me Samuel, what brings you downtown?" Joseph asked.

Samuel glanced at Devorah and Rachel before looking Joseph in the eyes. "Saul has me running a few errands. I saw you in the market." Joseph stopped chewing his sandwich and looked at Samuel. *Had he been the one who'd followed him?*

"Sorry, I must have missed you."

"You did," Samuel said, running a hand over his mustache, "but that might have been a good thing, because it looked like someone *else* was following you." Joseph put the sandwich down this time. "Don't worry, you were in no danger; like I said, Saul asked me to run a few errands." Samuel smiled at him.

"I could feel someone watching me. I ducked into the market and hotel to lose him."

"Well I'm glad to see it worked, but you lost me in the process. I'm just glad I know the area, and I figured that I would stop by to see Widow Douglas."

"You see, Rachel! I told you that those silly names would stick."

"We were just kids, Mamma—how were we to know that everyone would keep calling us by those names? Why was someone following Joseph?"

Samuel leaned forward in his char. "It's nothing too bad, and I was probably mistaken anyways, but right now the king would like Joseph to be careful and keep a low profile. He knows he has your trust." Devorah and Rachel both nodded in acceptance.

Devorah gripped the top of Joseph's hand, "We have an extra room that you can stay in as long as you like. We will take good care of—" She looked around the table. ". . . of our Little John." Rachel burst out laughing as Joseph and Samuel chuckled.

Rachel pointed at Samuel, who was again flattening his mustache, "Don't you think that Samuel would have made a good Injun Joe?"

Joseph smiled at her. "I don't think that Tom or Huck could have competed with a *French* Injun Joe. You know what kind of reputation those Frenchmen have with the girls? Becky Thatcher would have turned Injun Joe's world upside down if he had wooed her with that French tongue of his."

Rachel looked at what was left on her plate. "I don't know. Becky had a pretty good head on her shoulders; I think she could have decided for herself."

Sighing, Rachel's mother rose to her feet. "I have heard quite enough of this foolishness at the table."

"Here is to good health and fortune, *osher uvree ut.*" Joseph raised his glass and finished his wine as Samuel replied

"*Bonne santé à vous!*" he toasted, repeating so that the widow could understand, "good health to you!" Finishing his glass he continued, "By the way Joseph, I am going to walk over to Jaffa and pick up some copies of a print that I have been working on for about two years. Would you like to walk with me?"

Joseph and Samuel excused themselves with assurances that they wouldn't be gone long. "Sorry to pull you away, it's only a short walk to the studio. Oh, and Eugene Delacroix is what E.D. stands for." Samuel lit a cigarette and spoke between puffs, the light grey smoke scattering in the wind. "The king said you had been interested in the painting in his bathroom. You have no idea how many times I've tried to get him to move it to somewhere a little more worthy of its station. Delacroix was thought to be one of the most important of the French Romantic painters. He died in Paris in 1863 and was buried in the Père Lachaise Cemetery. The next time I return to Paris you will have to come along. We can visit the Louvre and see all of the great works."

"It would be an honor. I have always wanted to see the *Mona Lisa*," Joseph replied.

"Ah yes, the *Mona Lisa*—the most famous painting in all of history. Quite extraordinary—they say it is the woman's smile that drives men mad trying to get inside her head." Samuel puffed on his cigarette and thought a moment before continuing, "I have seen that smile several times today on Rachel's lips when she is looking at you."

Joseph stopped in his tracks, and Samuel turned, laughing at him. "Love is only difficult to see when you are its target, my friend."

"Samuel, we've known each other ever since we were kids," Joseph said.

"That's my point exactly! Are you blind? From what I have heard, you have always been her knight in shining armor."

"She thinks of me as an older brother." Joseph had begun walking again, and he was finding it difficult to look into Samuel's eyes.

"Like I said, its target is always blind. I don't think that's how Rachel sees you."

"You are wrong my friend. Maybe before, when we were children . . ." Tantalizing images from his dreams drifted through his head, and the feeling of lips pressed against his cheek, warm against the cold. Shaking his head, he looked at Samuel. "I struggle to remember what it was like to be a child, to have grown up with Rachel, and my memories are mixed with fantasy and imagination. It's hard to even sort through my *own* mind without knowing hers."

"OK, OK, Joseph," Samuel smiled at him. "It's just something I noticed, but don't be surprised if she takes advantage of having you in her home for a few days."

As they entered the print shop, Samuel was immediately recognized and greeted by the proprietor, who ducked into the back and returned with a long cylindrical tube; he handed it over. As Samuel pulled and unrolled the print from the tube, Joseph recognized the print as a scene depicting an old Masonic ritual.

"It's beautiful, Samuel."

"The true beauty of a work is always difficult for the artist to see. We see the brushstrokes that we did not complete, the shapes not perfect, or color just a little off hue, but—" Samuel deftly returned the print to its casing and grabbed Joseph's arm. ". . . if we are not able to get past seeing the imperfections of our ability, we can never understand that the world sees our missing strokes, our off colors, as what *makes* the masterpiece."

When they returned back to Widow Douglas's home, Rachel was just finishing with helping her mother tidy up the kitchen and dining area. After noticing their return, Rachel took some fresh strawberries from the fridge.

"Would you guys like some coffee to go with the strawberries and cream?"

Samuel and Joseph consented in unison.

As Rachel handed the crystal dessert dishes filled with the fresh strawberries to Joseph and poured coffee, Samuel stepped out onto the porch to make a call.

"So, what did you and Samuel talk about on your little walk together? Don't think we didn't notice you didn't invite us."

Joseph looked at her raised eyebrow, the way that it fell into the curve of her face, ending in a smile at her lips. "Art."

Rachel leaned back on her hip, "Art, really? Not more information about who was following you, or information from Saul, or *anything* about your injuries at an important time like this?"

"Nope, just—art." With a sigh, Rachel placed the coffees and desserts on a plate and waved Joseph out the door toward the patio.

Although the courtyard had only about half a dozen trees or so, there was some shade, and this made the courtyard a little cooler. Samuel gladly took his coffee and strawberries and sat at a small old gazebo available only to the residents. "The king has agreed that you should stay here. He trusts your safety here over a hotel."

"I appreciate the king's concern, but I really don't think it is necessary."

"Well I don't think it is either, but the king has asked me to tell you to do so. If questions come up you will say you are having renovations done, but stay out of sight as much as possible. If you do need to go out, put on a cap and glasses, something to cover you. Someone *was* following you, Joseph, I'm sure of it."

"Are we blaming renovations now for trying to stay over at my house, Joseph?" Rachel had joined them.

"If you are worried about it, I can find somewhere else to stay."

Rachel abruptly turned with defiance and went back inside. Joseph sighed as the door shut behind her.

Samuel chuckled, "She *really* likes you, Achi, but I don't know exactly why."

"I think I'll need that hat and glasses now."

"Oh?" Samuel opened his bag and handed over the items.

"I think I need to buy some flowers." Samuel leaned back, lit a cigarette, and laughed.

11

According to his royally issued cell phone it was about five-fifteen when Joseph made his way down the pedestrian mall. There were still plenty of vendors set up. This was the best time to get a good deal as the merchants haggled viciously, working to make a bit more profit before the day's end. It took Joseph about forty minutes, but he made his way over to the Christian Quarter and the Muristan area. The Muristan area included the Avtimos market and the German Church of the Redeemer, a beautiful brownstone-and-brick church that was built over the Church of St. Mary of the Latins. There is also speculation that the Church of St. Mary was built over an even earlier church, which may have stood over the same location as early as the fifth century. The current church of the Redeemer had a beautiful bell tower that offered a view as far away as the Mount of Olives and Mount Zion.

Joseph also knew that there were several jewelry shops located close by. He was familiar with one in particular. It was the SeTed jewelry shop, on Dabbagha Street. They sold all kinds of high-end jewelry and watches. The proprietor, David Weinberg, was an old school friend of his. He and Joseph had gone to school together for many years, before David's father died and he had dropped out to take over the family business. Joseph tried to think of the last time that he and David had gotten together. He knew that they hadn't talked much in a couple of years.

When he arrived, it appeared they were getting ready to close. A young black-headed teenage girl sat behind the counter in the front. When Joseph first looked into the shop from the outside, he could see that she had begun to pull the trays of rings and necklaces from the counter and take them to the back. As Joseph stepped inside, she looked up. "I'm sorry but we will be closing shortly. If there was anything I can help you with, just let me know."

"Actually, I'm here to see David."

The girl looked him over and walked to the back. Joseph was leaning over the counter, looking at the watches in the case, when he heard a voice shout from the back.

"Oh my God, I can't believe my eyes. Can it be?" Joseph looked up and saw David standing in the doorway. "It is so good to see you my friend," David said. "How long has it been?"

"It has been too long and I am so sorry to hear about your father's passing."

"Yes, we still miss him a lot. Don't we, Rivee?" David was looking at the young women working in his shop. As Joseph looked at the young woman, he realized that it was David's daughter.

"Rivee? Is this Rivka?" he asked.

"Yes, Joseph, this is my little Rivka, but she prefers Rivee. You know how teenagers are." Joseph just shook his head and looked at her.

"I can't believe how you have grown. The last time I saw you, you were only about three feet tall" he said.

David introduced his daughter to Joseph, telling her about the king's palace and the new temple being built on the mountain.

"So, Joseph, what brings you around? I know you just didn't stop by to shop, did you?" David asked.

"Is there somewhere we can talk?" Joseph asked. David nodded to Rivee, who continued with closing the shop, and led Joseph to the back office and living quarters. Joseph sat down in a chair opposite David at a half moon–shaped desk. After a few minutes of small talk, Joseph explained to David the real reason he was there. "David, do you remember the jewel that King Oman presented to me several years ago?" David assured him that he did. "Well, I have misplaced it and was wondering if I could get the radio tracking frequency. That is, if you have it."

"Oh yes, I have it." David rose, moved back to the storefront, and returned with a small black box of index cards. "After I did your jewel, I began offering the service; apparently more people than you would expect loved the idea. Our little conversation has turned into a niche market for me, and it has earned me quite a few pennies." He pulled a card out and flourished it with a smile before jotting down the number on a business card, which he handed over to Joseph. Now all Joseph would have to do was provide the king with the number.

After bidding his friend goodbye, and promising to call for coffee, Joseph headed back to King George Street and his temporary quarters. He picked up a nice pastel bouquet of daisies, mums, and safflower for the house. It wasn't much, but he was sure that Rachel and her mother would appreciate them. The widow had always liked flowers. Joseph had heard her say, on more than one occasion, that "flowers were always beautiful, never critical, and could express clearly their message without ever having to say a word." When Joseph got back to King George Street it was close to ten o'clock. He didn't really expect to find anyone still up and was surprised to find Rachel watching reruns of *The Wonder Years* on TV.

As he sat down on the sofa next to Rachel, he noticed the light from the screen flickering against her skin, and shining in her eyes. She looked at him and smiled. "Do you want something to drink?"

He shook his head. "No, I just want to get some rest. Which room will I be sleeping in?"

Slumping back in the couch, she returned her attention to the TV. "I think my mother wants you to use the room downstairs. She put clean sheets on the bed a little earlier, and laid out some fresh towels. I can show you the way if you'd like."

"I . . ." Joseph looked at her, her feet tucked beneath her, the shadows accentuating her angular features. "I'll be all right." Moving quickly, he made his way down the stairs to a small room that looked as though it had been made as a bomb shelter. There were no windows, no sink, and no bed. He didn't see any fresh towels either. He went back upstairs and found her still watching TV. Before he could even begin she stopped him. "You went down the wrong stairs." She laughed and reminded Joseph that he had always gone down the wrong set as a child.

"I don't remember that." They looked at each other for a moment, and in that pause Rachel rose and hugged him.

"There are a lot of things I wish you could remember, but I guess I'll just have to take you as you are, Little John. Come on, I'll show you the other stairs." Rachel led Joseph down the small hallway toward the rear of the house. As they were about to go out of the back door she turned left toward what looked like a small closet. "Here we go," she said.

"What is this?"

"This is your room." As Joseph opened the door, Rachel switched on the stairwell light. There was a small stairway that led down about twelve or fourteen steps.

"I never knew a room was down there."

"Yeah you did," she said, glancing at him out of the corner of her eye, "you just forgot. Probably forgot a lot of what we did as kids down here, but it's pretty neat, huh? There's even a bath," she added. She let him survey the room, remaining at the base of the stairs. "Joseph, do you ever wish you could turn back the clock and relive those days again?"

Joseph stared at the towels on the bed, running his hands over the coarse wool. He answered with his back toward her, "Of course I do. Sometimes, I dream about it, and I can't tell which part is memory and which is imagination." With a sigh he closed and rubbed his eyes. It was late, and he needed real sleep. "Rachel, I just wanted to say thanks. I really appreciate everything that you and your mother are doing for me," Joseph turned back just in time to see the door closing at the top of the stairs.

As he lay in bed, Joseph listened to the quiet of the room. This was quite a change from lying in a dug-out dirt hole in the catacombs. The bed was soft and clean, and it carried the smell of bread and lilacs. As Joseph lay there thinking about the events of the last two days, he couldn't help but remember a little prayer that he used to say each night as he got in bed.

Now I lay me down to sleep, I pray the Lord my soul to keep, if I should die before I wake, I pray the Lord my soul to take. It was a comforting prayer and one that always reminded him of his youth. It was also a time when his biggest problems could always be solved by his mother giving him a kiss on the cheek and a hug around the neck. Slowly he closed his eyes, and he was instantly asleep. He dreamed of home-cooked meals from his mother, and of running through caves with Saul, and of the warmth of a kiss against his cheek on a cold night.

When he awoke the next morning, he could not believe that he had slept the entire night. He lay still for a few moments, just soaking in the warmth of the bed as the dreams faded, unwillingly, away. He was just about to get up when he heard the ascending beeping tones of his cell phone ringing somewhere over the horizon of the bed. With minimal effort he let his arm fall over the edge and scan the floor with no result until the phone finally gave up. Ten seconds later, it resumed its call, and although he knew it was impossible, the ring seemed louder.

"Just answer the damn thing." Joseph froze. It was Rachel's voice. Joseph sat up and looked beside him where Rachel was lying.

"Uh, good morning? I don't remember you being here when I fell asleep."

She shrugged as she sat up and began arranging her hair. "I was lonely. You were muttering in your sleep by the way." Seeing the look on Joseph's face, she laughed. "Get that look off your face! And you don't need to whisper—it's just like when we were kids."

"Rachel, look around—we are not kids anymore!" Joseph could still hear the cell phone ringing and he could hear himself getting a little too loud.

Rachel set her jaw and rose to a sitting position. "I know that, Joseph, but it was night, and we were both under this roof again, and I . . . I just wanted to be here. I know you don't remember everything, but I do, and I'm not forgetting it." Getting up and out of bed, Joseph could see that she was well covered in her pajamas. She scooped up the phone and glanced at the number. "It's Saul." She accepted the call as she walked up the stairs and opened the door, leaving the smell of lilacs behind her. With a sigh, Joseph got up, used the bathroom, washed his face, dressed, and followed Rachel upstairs where breakfast was already on the table. There were crepes filled with cheese and fruit, some more fresh strawberries, hot coffee, and juice.

"*Boker Tov*," Joseph said to her as he sat down.

"And a good morning to you. Did you sleep well?" the widow asked.

Joseph looked her in the eyes and swallowed, "It was the best night's sleep I have had in years. I slept all night long. In fact I don't remember waking up a single time, not once, all night." he said.

"A simple yes or no would have been sufficient."

"Sorry, yes, I slept well, thank you." The crepes proved a deterrent to putting his foot in his mouth any deeper.

Rachel appeared from the bathroom and sat down. As Devorah shoveled food onto her plate she asked, "And how did you sleep, Rachel?"

To Joseph's surprise and shock, Rachel smiled. "I slept great and I fell asleep with good ol' Huck Finn."

Joseph nearly choked. Devorah shook her head as she walked back to the kitchen. "Why do you always have your nose in those old books? Don't you ever read anything new?" Joseph took a long drink of coffee to force the crepes down.

"What's the matter, Huck? You looked like you're surprised at my choice of literature." Rachel's smile was wicked. "Oh, by the way, here's your phone back, Joseph. You know, from when you let me borrow it when we woke up." With that, Rachel excused herself from the table, pulling her own phone from her pocket. "I have to make a call if you'll excuse me."

Joseph didn't respond. He didn't even look at Rachel. If Devorah suspected anything, she certainly did not let on. Then again, she was used to Rachel's colorful remarks. Joseph tried to finish eating quickly, keeping his eyes on his plate, before he excused himself and headed out the door. He pulled out the cell phone and dialed Saul. It only rang once before it was answered.

"Good morning, Huck, how was breakfast?"

Joseph sighed, "Well it's pretty obvious you know exactly how my breakfast was, Your Majesty."

"Joseph, can I put you on hold for a minute? I have someone else on the other line."

"Your Majesty, please tell Rachel that I don't like surprises, especially when I'm waking up in the morning."

Joseph walked another twenty-five or thirty feet before the king reconnected.

"I am sorry; I was talking with one of my old childhood friends. Can you stop by? I have news I think will interest you."

"I can be there in about twenty minutes."

"OK, Achi, I'll see you in about twenty minutes then." Joseph closed his phone and slipped it back into his pocket. He stopped walking and turned and looked back. He could see Rachel. She was standing outside on the porch, with a phone to her ear; as he turned she waved casually and walked back into the house.

12

As Joseph continued up the street, he heard the morning prayers that were once again being broadcast throughout the city over the PA system. Today was the Sabbath and many people were already out and about. It was also the Feast of the Tabernacle. The streets were filled with many Jews and Christians who'd come from all over the world. The locals were out on the streets too. They just wanted to watch. For Christians this was a feast of joy, and a time for them to strengthen their relationship with their creator.

As Joseph made his way through the street, he overheard several locals talking about the two boys who had been killed the night before in Sderot, less than a mile from Gaza. In recent months, there had been several Palestinian rocket attacks fired by Hamas and the Islamic Jihad. Finding a news stand, Joseph stuck his hand in his pocket, pulled out some loose change, and purchased a morning paper to see what everyone was talking about.

There was the picture, right on the front page. It showed two young boys lying next to each other in a pool of blood, sprawled out on a sidewalk in Sderot. Joseph began to read about the two brothers. One was nineteen, and the other was eight. They had borrowed their mother's credit card to go to the ATM machine; they were going to get money to buy some shaving lotion as a birthday present for their father. When the warning sirens sounded, they ran for their lives. But they couldn't escape; they were killed by shrapnel from a Hamas rocket. Joseph continued to read how pieces of the eldest boy's legs were found scattered on the street. One of the younger boy's legs was severed; the other had been shattered by the blast. The paper quoted one of the local residents saying that, "The closest shelter was only about one hundred meters away." Continuing on to the next page, Joseph read that the Qassam rocket that struck the village was believed to be a simple steel rocket filled with common tools and scrap, which were propelled using a solid mixture of sugar and potassium nitrate (widely used as a fertilizer).

Before Joseph knew it, he had made his way across town and was just outside the palace. He slipped the paper under his arm and made his way into a small alleyway and to a side entrance where he rang the buzzer. After a few minutes the door opened, and Phillip greeted him once again.

"Hello sir, this way please, the king is waiting for you." This time Phillip escorted him through the main kitchen area into the rear courtyard. There were beautiful flowers, trees, and shrubs of every variety imaginable decorating every inch. White marble stone footpaths separated each section. From the courtyard they walked northwest to a small entryway leading into what Joseph referred to as "the west wing." Upon entering, it opened into a vast sports arena.

A full-sized basketball court was adjacent to an Olympic-sized swimming pool. The outer edge of the floor had doorways into the weight rooms, fencing area, and sauna. Above all of this, along the perimeter wall was a quarter-mile track that encircled the entire complex. The king was currently running laps. All of this was in a climate-controlled environment underneath a state-of-the-art retractable roof. The roof had magnificent fresco paintings on different sections depicting various biblical scenes. Behind each scene, the starry-decked heavens were painted to cover the roof. Joseph was in awe every time that he visited and knew that there wasn't anything like it anywhere, except of course the Sistine Chapel. This was Samuel's work, and it was breathtaking. The king's arena was the largest building in the area, second only to the Nokia Arena in Israel. Phillip led Joseph across the court into the locker room. There, he had already laid out a set of running shoes, shorts, socks, and shirt.

"The king asked that you join him, sir" advised Phillip. Just then, Joseph's cell phone rang again. It was the king.

"Joseph, if you hurry and change, you can catch me on my next pass."

"I'll just be a minute or two, Your Majesty." Joseph hurriedly changed and ran up the steps to the track landing. After stretching out, Joseph started jogging around the track. Soon the king had caught up and together they ran another six or seven laps before they stopped. Joseph had worked up a good sweat, and his heart was pounding.

"How many laps did you run, Your Majesty?" he asked.

"I'm not sure, I think about twenty. We'll have to look at the video to make sure," the king replied.

"You were running when I first called then? I thought you sounded a little out of breath," Joseph observed.

The king preferred to run on natural trails, but with his schedule it was almost impossible. After the run, Joseph took a hot shower, got dressed, and waited for the king in a side room just off from his chambers. The neat thing about being the architect was that Joseph pretty much knew where everything was located. A bowl of mixed fruit had been set out for him, along with several bottles of cold water. Joseph guessed that Phillip had set them out. He grabbed a few grapes and opened a bottle of water before the king entered and motioned to join him in the study.

The study was two flights up and had a bay window that overlooked the mountain region. The walls were a high, glossy, dark mahogany, as was the desk where the king was now sitting. The king's desk was magnificent. It had been given to him by King Hussein bin Talal during a week-long visit. Joseph remembered it well because he had been commissioned to completely redo the entire room to match the gift. It was widely know that King Hussein was a Past Grand Master of the Grand Lodge of Jordan.

As the king sat down, he leaned back in his chair and took a piece of paper from the center desk drawer and placed it in front of him. Joseph was standing near the desk but was still looking out the bay window toward the mountain region. Neither of them said anything for a few moments. Finally, the king invited Joseph to sit down and asked if he would like a cup of coffee.

"Yes, that would be great," Joseph said. The king swiveled his chair, and there was a silver carafe sitting on a tray behind his desk.

"I had this brought in earlier. Café mocha. It is quite good. I admit I've acquired a taste for it."

Joseph reached for the cup and took a sip. As Joseph sipped his coffee, King Oman picked up the piece of paper and slid it across the desk.

"Joseph, there is a single name written on this piece of paper. It is the name of the individual that has caused us so much anguish." Staring at the paper, Joseph asked the king what he proposed that they do.

"That, Achi, is what we must decide," replied the king. As Joseph reached for the note, the king asked,

"Are you sure you want to know their name?" Joseph's hand stopped moving.

"That is a very good question, Your Majesty."

"This is not about you or me, Joseph. This is much, much bigger. This is about morals, principles, and obligations. It's about duty, honor, and dignity. It is about how the principles of one man can affect the lives of many. This is an issue of trust, and also one of betrayal," he said. "But it's more than this, Joseph. This is about freedom and courage, both yours and mine. Do you understand?" asked the king.

"I'm not sure, Your Majesty." The king leaned his head back on his chair, gazed up at the ceiling, and said, "OK, let me see if I can explain." After a short pause the king asked, "Joseph how is your Latin?"

"My Latin, Your Majesty?" replied Joseph.

"Yes, how is your Latin?" asked the king.

"It could use some polish but it's not bad. I was able to read the inscription on the floor in the spa without any difficulty. I believe it said, 'Blessed is the man who finds wisdom.'"

"Yes, that's right. Proverbs, you know. A paraphrase from 3:13," replied the king. "Then," the king asked, "you are familiar with the word *traditorem*?"

Joseph answered, "*Traditorem*? Let's see. I think so. I believe it has something to do with traitor."

"Yes! Correct again. Very good. This man, whose name I have written on this piece of paper, is a man who I believe falls into the category of *traditorem*, or betrayer. In other words he is under what I refer to as the Judas Syndrome. Now I know you are familiar with this term?"

Joseph answered, "I am familiar with the name Judas and what it has come to mean."

"The Judas Syndrome is a term that many use to categorize individuals who betray the one closest to them for personal gain. I have seen this in every circle, at every level, and in every country. I am never surprised to learn that someone has been sold out by an individual who has been invited within their so-called inner circle." King Oman continued, "You know Joseph, when a person is betrayed, at first they don't want to believe it. They try to figure out why it happened. Then they feel foolish that they didn't see it coming." King Oman got up from the desk and walked over to the bay window and looked toward the mountains.

"It's a disease, Joseph. In most cases the person who decides that they are going to betray never realizes that they are doing it. The Judas rationalizes every single thing that they do. They are never in conflict with themselves because they have but one goal: to achieve that which they cannot get or have by legitimate means. They are never regretful or apologetic. These people are usually always jealous, they lack faith, they are impatient, narrow-minded, and they are completely narcissistic. Thus the Judas Syndrome, which we have come to know so well." Joseph once again reached for the piece of paper. This time the king did not say a thing. Joseph held the paper in his hand for several minutes gripping it tightly. Finally, slowly, Joseph unfolded the paper and looked at the name that had been written down. He read the name silently and then folded it and placed it back on the king's desk. The king watched, surprised that Joseph showed no sign of emotion.

The king picked up the note from his desk and said, "Joseph, it doesn't appear that either one of us is too surprised by learning who our nemesis is." Joseph looked up at the king.

"Why should it be any different for us, Your Majesty? If it can happen to a simple carpenter, it can happen to anyone."

"You're right, it isn't any different as far as I am concerned, Joseph. And there are almost as many players in this plot as the one that took place in the garden at Gethsemane."

"Your Majesty, what about the other players involved? Surely we have identified the ones at the compound by now."

"No, Achi, I'm afraid not yet."

"Are we sure that they worked at the compound?"

The king responded, "Joseph, they are of no concern. You and I have been betrayed by but one person. Our Judas has no regard for the petals contained within the White Rose of our brotherhood. All the other people participating are under his influence and either cannot or do not have the capacity to think for themselves. Do not worry, Achi.

Once we force his hand, all who are involved will be made known and will be judged accordingly," replied the king.

"What happens then, Your Majesty?" Joseph asked.

"Only God will know the answer to that, Achi." Joseph remembered the newspaper and retrieved it from his back pocket.

"Your Majesty, have you seen today's paper? There were two young boys killed in Sderot last evening."

Looking down at his lap, the king nodded his head. "Yes Joseph, I have seen the papers, and the news caught the air strikes. The HLN are already running them on television. I spoke with the boys' family last night and expressed my condolences, for all the good that a king can do for those he has failed. I have already been in contact with the Israeli Defense Ministry and with allied forces pertaining to these and other air strikes. We are all trying to come up with a plan to combat Hamas air strikes and rockets. All around us, Joseph, are people who target our kingdom, and all we can do is work hard and keep our faith."

Joseph looked at Saul, sitting with his hands clasped and eyes closed. Saul was all that Joseph would want Israel to be. Saul opened his eyes and looked at his friend. "In the epistle to the Hebrews, it says, 'Faith is the substance of things hoped for, the evidence of things not seen.' Let us have faith in each other, and in our people, to weather this crisis."

The king got up, walked over to where Joseph was standing, and placed both of his hands on his shoulders as he looked him in the face. "I have known men and women of faith, who are all caring men and women of God, who live each day with one thought in mind: to love one another. This Judas and these other men who have betrayal in their hearts are not any of those things." Saul was scrutinizing him. "You know what I think, Joseph?"

"What is that, Your Majesty?"

"I think that you are under the impression that what has happened is somehow your fault. Let me tell you this: sometimes things happen and neither you, nor I, have any control. This was, and is, one of those times. You have done nothing wrong, Achi."

As the king continued to speak, Joseph's thoughts turned toward Rachel. For some reason he found himself wanting to see her again and he didn't know why.

"Joseph, are you all right?"

"I am fine. I just have several things on my mind."

The king smiled. "I can have Phillip prepare one of the guest rooms for you to stay in for as long as you wish."

Joseph bowed his head slightly. "I really appreciate your hospitality, but I have already made arrangements with Widow Douglas. I will just stay there for a while." Again, the king smiled and asked him to convey his regards to the "widow" and to Rachel. What Joseph did not want to tell the king was that he could not get Rachel out of his mind. He was thinking of a more innocent time. It had been good to see her after so long. Finding himself in the same bed as her had shocked him, and it had been quite innocent, but even thinking about it filled him with . . . what? Happiness? Longing?

"Are you listening?"

"I am sorry, Your Majesty," The king's question jolted Joseph back from his daydreaming. "I was just thinking about those three guys at the compound."

"Right, have you had any luck with getting the frequency on the necklace?"

"Yes, Your Majesty. I wrote it down on a piece of paper. I've got it right here."

The king picked up the phone and grabbed the card from Joseph's hand. The phone could only have rung once. "Commander Asaad, good news. We have the frequency number for the chip. Are you ready to copy?" As the caller rattled off the numbers, the king listened, and a grin spread across his face. "Thank you, Commander. That is good news. Please give my regards to Sophia."

"They were able to triangulate a signal coming from the mountains near Budrus. It is transmitting a signal that corresponds with the locator chip of the jewel. I'm going to make a few more calls, get some men out there. Either *your attackers* will be on site, or we will have a location to set a trap. Right now, they have anonymity from the law, but Joseph, we have the defense forces, and Asaad is a man like me." The king winked. "We don't let ourselves be bested in our own homes." Joseph could only imagine what the king had planned.

13

"Now, Joseph, I need for you to go away for a couple of days—to Haifa. You can meet with the Selleg Architects, and find out if they can give you a completion date for construction on the temple. I won't let these thugs disrupt the running of my country." The construction firm's main office was located in the northern region in Haifa on the Mediterranean coast.

"Your Majesty, I could get the completion date by picking up the phone—I don't see any reason for you to fly me out of the country."

The king took a seat behind his desk and rested his head on the thumbs of his steepled hands. "Samuel told me that you were followed in the market."

Joseph nodded. "I'm sorry I didn't bring it up sooner. I had assumed I was just being paranoid until Samuel assured me of it."

"Well, he didn't tell you the whole story either." Joseph's eyes widened as he waited for the king to continue.

"He was military, Joseph; of course Samuel didn't know who he was, but he took a picture before he lost track of him, and you. I had Phillip look at it with me. He was wearing civilian clothes, but the boots he was wearing, along with the belt and combat knife, were military issue. It's not too far-fetched to think that our enemy has at least some clout in our defense forces. If only we had gotten a picture of his face—even a side shot—we could identify him and have him interrogated. Even that might not be enough evidence."

"Joseph, I feel impotent. We know who our enemy is, with great assurance, yet if I see him I will smile and shake his hand. I cannot simply jail him like a common criminal; I need undeniable proof. Even if we had a confession from your pursuer it would be one man's word against another's. We need your attackers, Achi. We need to know the full plan. I have an idea, but we need to keep you out of sight, especially near or around the compound."

The phone was again in the king's hands. "Joseph, you're getting out of the city, and we need to make it harder to track you. I don't think that this threat is fully realized yet, otherwise I probably wouldn't still have the throne. I doubt he has the manpower to seriously track you beyond the city. Now, how do you feel about that trip to Haifa?" Joseph was about to open his mouth, but he realized it was rhetorical.

Joseph tried not to let it show, but just the word *vacation* sounded amazing. He needed a break to let his body and mind get centered. "When do I leave, Your Majesty?"

"Immediately," smiled the king. "I'll have Phillip pack you a bag. If you need anything else you can purchase it when you get there. Here, take this." The king had handed Joseph his black American Express card. "One of my most trusted operatives will accompany you to Haifa. They'll make sure that you are not bothered, and they'll be there to keep you informed as things progress while you are away. Should I need to contact you I'll use the cell. Don't go home, and don't go back to Devorah's; they're probably being watched. Now that we know he has some military personnel, who knows what other information he has. It was a lucky break you escaped the first time."

Saul had a look in his eyes that Joseph had seen many times before; he was controlling the frantic energy that he kept inside him, allowing only his worries and fears to show themselves as productive acts. It was a talent he had since his youth, and one that both elevated and alienated him in his already isolated station. "Saul, this operative, it isn't Phillip is it?"

The king blinked. "Phillip?"

Joseph smiled. "Yes, he informed me earlier that he's your combat specialist."

The king looked at Joseph and barked a laugh. "No," he advised, "If I were to send Phillip, who would be around to make my tea! I'm afraid you'll just have to wait until your flight, more information will be provided once you're onboard. I *will*, however, have Phillip drive you to the airport." With the flip of his phone, the king relayed the information to Phillip before turning back to Joseph. "I plan on making a trip to that location outside Budrus—we found the grave, Achi. You have no idea how lucky we are to have that location, all thanks to you. With a little luck it will be a turning point for our cause."

The king then held out his right hand, which Joseph took, and the two put their arms around each other's shoulders as the king whispered into his friend's ear. A knock at the door alerted them to Phillip's reappearance. With the phone back in his hand, Joseph lost the king to affairs of state; he then made his way out of the office, greeting Phillip in the hall.

He dialed Rachel as they made their way to the garage, where Phillip selected one of the king's cars. It was one thing not to go back to her home, but so many thoughts had been swirling through his head, it was quite another to not call her. He wanted to thank her and her mother for keeping him, and to tell her that he would be out of town; most importantly, he just wanted to talk to her. As Joseph climbed into the car, Rachel's voicemail picked up.

"Hello, this is Rachel, I'm sorry I am unavailable. Please leave your name and number and I will call you back."

"Hey Rachel, Joseph here, I am going to be away for a while at a meeting in Haifa. Please convey my deepest thanks to your mother, and tell her how much I appreciated her hospitality. I'll give you another call when I land. I really enjoyed seeing you again—hopefully we can do a little more of it in the future." Joseph flipped the phone shut and settled in for the forty-minute ride to the airport, which would make the drive a longer trip than the flight to Haifa once they were airborne.

The king chose exquisite vehicles—the same way he did everything else. This was a 2008 Mercedes-Benz S600 Pullman Limo. Joseph pulled the car description from the backseat flap and began to read. *This car is ridiculous.* Looking at the specifications Joseph read the manufacturers guide, "If you're worried about rifle projectiles and shrapnel from hand grenades, you might want to rethink your line of work. But, in the meantime, it is suggested you buy the new Mercedes-Benz S600 Pullman. Designed for dictators and dignitaries alike, the Pullman hosts an over abundance of luxury and security features you cannot find anywhere else."

Joseph glanced at the tinted plastiglass around him. "Phillip, do you know what you are driving?" Joseph continued to read. 'The most remarkable aspect of the Pullman is that it is designed to withstand a terrorist attack. It is rated at the highest protection level, which means it is able to withstand military style rifles and explosives. It has a 5.5-liter V-12 engine that produces 510 horsepower.' Phillip, this is not a car, this is a tank!"

"Yes sir, it surely is. Would you like to read today's paper?" Phillip asked as he handed the paper back to Joseph.

"Yes, thanks. Shall I give you a run down?" asked Joseph.

"Thank you, sir; I haven't had a chance to read it yet." Joseph began to read.

"OK, let's see, on the front page, a photo of Prime Minister Olmert with President Shimon Peres sitting together at the president's home in Jerusalem. Also, from Pakistan, a suicide bomber kills forty-eight and destroys a Pakistani mosque." Sighing, Joseph dropped the paper into his lap, crumpling the edges in his grip. "Phillip, just wake me up when we get to the airport."

"Very well, sir," replied Phillip.

14

After a brief nap, Joseph awoke looking onto the tarmac, their car slowing to a stop next to another black Mercedes of the same model. The king's plane was already waiting for them in the staging area. As Joseph exited the limo, he found that Phillip had already grabbed the luggage from the trunk and was walking it to the cargo area.

"I'll see you when you get back, sir. Have a nice flight!" he shouted over his shoulder. Joseph waved at him as he climbed up the stairs and stepped onto the plane. *Saul, can't you ever stop surprising me with your luxury?* This was not his first flight on the king's personal jet, but he was always amazed to see how the other half lived.

It looked like a miniature version of a media theater, a trend started by the *nouveau riche* several years ago. The dot-com generation had begun to include home theaters when building their trophy mansions. The seats were light tan and were glove-leather soft. Each chair seat held a goose down pillow encased in Egyptian cotton with the king's monogram embroidered in gold silk thread. At the front of the passenger area was a forty-two inch flat screen mounted to the wall and a small library of the latest movies on Blu-ray.

Joseph claimed his seat by settling in with his newest copy of *Runner's World*. There was a single seat on the opposite side of the plane, diagonal from his. In the back of the passenger section Joseph could see heavy drapes concealing another area, and voices (muted by soft background music) drifted from behind the curtains. From behind the drapes a young, attractive Israeli flight attendant appeared with a bottle of Cristal champagne and two baccarat crystal flutes.

"Good afternoon, sir, welcome aboard. My name is Hadashah. Please make yourself comfortable. We'll be taking off in about ten minutes. I'll be taking care of you on our flight. Would you care for a flute of Cristal?" As Hadashah asked Joseph about the champagne he noticed the second flute. Over Hadashah's shoulder, he could see the rear drape slide open again, and his heart jumped into his throat as a familiar voice greeted him.

"Good afternoon Joseph. Thank you, Hadashah, I will take it from here." As Hadashah returned to the back of the plane, despite the voice, he didn't recognize the woman that approached him at all. Short blonde hair hovered in bangs over her bright blue eyes. She was wearing what looked like a tan safari jacket and sports jeans, which Joseph followed down to her brown, leather, flat sling-back sandals.

"Do you like it?" Again, he recognized the voice, so he was sure he knew this person beyond doubt. She pointed to each piece as she made her way down her body. "Armani jacket, Sahara jeans, boot-cut of course, and these sandals are Manolo Blahnik. And you, Joseph, have your mouth open." She flicked the end of a silk scarf into his face before wrapping it around her neck. Hearing his own name he knew for certain, and the outline of her face stood out through her disguise as the inevitable smell of lilacs drifted to him.

"You can change your looks all you want, Rachel, but until you change your perfume it's not much of a disguise."

"Yeah right, you were gawking at a blonde beauty," she quipped.

"Are you the special operative accompanying me to Haifa?"

Rachel poured the champagne into the flutes. "Well, try not to act so surprised; you know that I've been working for the I.S.F. for years."

"I've had my suspicions, but I never knew for sure. Some things you just don't ask. Where did you get those blue eyes?"

She laughed. "Do you like them? The contacts came with the wig. You would be surprised at just how versatile I can be."

Joseph shook his head. "I believe it, but it looks like you're going on a safari. This is how you dress?"

"You would be surprised how many times a good disguise has helped me get out of something."

Joseph chuckled, "What, like when you had to get close to someone who liked blond girls?"

Rachel's eyes seared him. "More like when people are told to look for a blonde, and I can rip off the wig and be brunette. It's faster to get out of a disguise than get into one, and it's saved me more than once."

Whoever said that it does not matter who you know was entirely wrong. Rachel had been assigned to the king while she was still in the army. All citizens, regardless of gender, had to serve, but not all who served were assigned to a detail with the king. The newly graduated high school students are whisked off to recruit training soon after their rites of passage. Women serve for a minimum of two years and men for three. Rachel was only going to serve the minimum time, but she took an interest in special operations. As it turned out, she was a natural soldier. She received a lot of encouragement from her superior officers; this led to her passage into the highly classified Special Forces unit of the Israeli Defense Force, the *Sayeret Matkal*.

Members were handpicked based on personal performance and nominations from existing members. This special unit that Rachel had been a part of—and still might be a member of, for all he knew—was known throughout the country for being the elite of the Israeli Army. Joseph first learned of the Special Forces Unit while he was serving in the regular army. He was turned off by the unit's grueling selection process and training that each potential recruit had to complete. It made the already grueling basic training seem like day camp. Once the new recruit was selected, he was sent to a secret location to receive specialized training in small arms, martial arts, navigation, camouflage, reconnaissance, and other skills that would help him survive behind enemy lines.

Before anyone was awarded the prestigious Red Beret, he was required to complete paratrooper training, two more months of advanced infantry training, three additional weeks of advanced parachute training, and finally five weeks of counter-terrorist training. All this training was then followed by more inner-unit drills. And just when a recruit thinks that he has made it and is getting ready to graduate, the military sends the recruits to long-range reconnaissance patrol. This is where the recruit participates in a long-range solo navigation exercise. It was also where the instructors get to mess with the recruits' minds. The irony in all of this is that even *after* they are awarded the title, members aren't allowed to even wear an insignia identifying them as a *Sayeret Matkal* due to its classified nature.

A voice spoke clearly from over the intercom, though the American accent was pronounced, "Welcome aboard flight 1151, from Jerusalem to Haifa. This is your Captain," he said. As the captain continued to give his preflight announcement, Joseph fastened his seatbelt. Rachel had sat down opposite Joseph, and she noticed as Joseph downed his entire flute in one swallow.

Rachel laughed, sipping on her glass, "Are you nervous, Joseph? I didn't think that you were afraid to fly, especially after all those jumps," Rachel remarked.

"Rachel. You know I am not afraid to fly. It's not the flying that has me worried, it's those unexpected crashes that bother me."

As the captain finished speaking, the cabin door was closed and the plane began its taxi down the runway. As they started moving, Joseph looked out the window and saw Phillip still parked on the tarmac, talking on his cell, probably letting the king know that the plane was departing safely.

Hadashah's voice sounded over the intercom, "I just wanted to remind you to make sure your seatbelts are secure and that you will need to stay in your seats. This will be a very short flight."

As the captain pulled back on the throttle, Joseph felt the inertial forces pushing him back into his seat. It only took about ten or eleven seconds for the plane to become airborne. Once off the ground, they quickly ascended and made a sharp bank toward Haifa. Joseph tried to relax back into his recliner and ignore how distracting it was with Rachel sitting directly across from him. She was on her cell, texting, and she occasionally glanced over. Joseph tried to ignore her by opening the April *Runner's World* and thumbing through the pages. "Please, give the king my regards."

Rachel ignored him, but a smile crept into the corner of her mouth as she continued her message. As the plane leveled off, the captain came back on the intercom. "Well, we are now traveling at approximately 460 knots, at twenty thousand feet. Clear skies ahead of us. We should be descending for our approach to Haifa in a little less than twenty minutes. As Joseph looked to his left, he could see the Mediterranean on the horizon. Closer in he could see some small communities but was unable to recognize any of them. Rachel had finished her text messaging and was now sitting back and gazing out the window. In the back, Joseph noticed Hadashah was up from her seat and moving about the plane. They locked eyes for a moment, and she gave him a friendly smile before closing the curtain. Almost all of the section was blocked off, and the hairs on his neck stood on end.

The blast that shook the plane was followed immediately by the depressurizing of the cabin, and Joseph felt the
plane roll to the side. His ears immediately filled with the
constant static buzz of air rushing past him. Joseph gripped
his seat and looked at Rachel, her blue eyes staring back
into his and her features unfazed. Magazines, blankets, and
DVDs were sucked out and into the rear of the plane. As
the curtains shielding the back section were ripped away,
Joseph could see that about half the tail section had been
torn away. Hadashah was nowhere in sight. He could see the
clear blue sky rocking back and forth as the pilots struggled
to keep the plane level as it lost altitude.

The captain burst through the cockpit door, gripping
the handrails, and approached Joseph. He had a parachute
strapped to his back. He thrust a chute into Joseph's arms,
shouting instructions above the deafening howl as air was
sucked out of the plane. Making a dive across the plane, and
batting dangling oxygen masks out of the way, he shoved
another chute into Rachel's arms.

"PUT THEM ON NOW!" Rachel slipped into the
chute like a second skin and moved to Joseph to help him.
"We are all going to jump! We only got about forty seconds
before the plane hits the ground! Once you are safely away
from the plane, pull the red ripcord on your chest!"

The co-pilot appeared, yelling and shaking his head
at the captain. In a snarl the captain grabbed Joseph and
Rachel by the back of their shirts and leapt.

As they jumped, Rachel pushed Joseph and the captain
away from her so that their chutes could deploy without
getting tangled. Images flashed before Joseph's eyes as the
ground rushed up to meet him. Images from his training and

missions crowded his focus as he tried to maintain a visual on Rachel. The captain had already pulled his chute, but he wanted to stay as close to Rachel in his timing as possible to be sure of where she landed. Realizing *she* was waiting on *him*, Joseph cursed and pulled his chord. As he fell, the canopy quickly opened and snapped into full position; he began his slow drift to the mountainside below. Looking up, he could see Rachel's canopy just above him.

From his estimate, they were only a couple hundred meters apart. Looking up and to his left, Joseph spotted two more canopies; it was the pilot and co-pilot. It looked as though they were headed higher up into the mountain region. As he continued his descent, Joseph saw the plane plummet toward the earth. It only looked as though it was about twelve to fifteen kilometers north from his position. As it hit, Joseph saw the explosion that bloomed out into the countryside, settling into a cloud of dirt and smoke that drifted over the site. The ground was coming up fast now. Trying to remember what he was supposed to do, Joseph bent his knees and rolled as the impact shook his bones. He came to a sudden stop, and his canopy fell directly on top of him. He quickly got up and checked for broken bones. *Thank God.*

As Joseph was taking stock he heard Rachel screaming his name, "JOSEPH!" She had landed just above him and was running down a footpath toward him. As she reached him, she grabbed him around the neck, squeezing him tightly.

"Rachel! RACHEL! Cut it out. Are you crazy?" Joseph shouted.

"Joseph, I'm sorry. I thought I had lost you. Are you all right?" she asked.

"I'm OK," Joseph said. "What the hell happened?"

"I don't know—did the pilots make it out?"

"They were drifting toward the mountains, maybe a few kilometers north of us."

"I didn't see Hadashah after the blast." Rachel scanned the smoke of the crash site.

"I don't think she made it out." They were quiet for a moment, and Joseph could feel Rachel's eyes on him. "Well, what now miss I.S.F.?" he said.

Rachel had her cell out and was typing quickly. "I have no idea how they found us; there aren't many options. Wait here, I'm checking in. As her call connected, she turned and walked a few meters away. Joseph could hear her reporting in terse statements, and the silence between her statements was filled with focus. It was either Saul or her commanders within the service.

They looked around their landing spot and found that the terrain was filled with rocks and crags that covered most of the countryside. He gave quick thanks, amazed that they had made it safely. Down the mountain, less than a kilometer, the ground filled with grasses—it was almost picturesque. Near the water, he could see a small village. Already, several people had gathered and were looking up in their direction.

As Rachel saw them she yelled down and waved her arms, "What is our location? Where are we?"

One young girl, hearing Rachel, ran into her home. A few seconds later, the young girl reappeared with an older man standing at her side, pointing up the hillside at them. Joseph immediately raised both of his arms above his head and waved their distress. The older gentleman jogged to a shed near the side of the home and reappeared in a small tractor. Slowly grinding up the countryside, he headed up the mountain in their direction. The young girl ran behind.

"We were really lucky." It was Rachel, still panting as she stood with her hands on her hips, watching the man's slow progression.

"Maybe it just wasn't our time to go." They'd somehow safely landed in a rock-covered field, and yet he didn't have a scratch. He'd received more injuries from the beating inflicted by those three thugs at the compound; they'd beaten him and left him for dead. Now he'd jumped out of a crashing airplane and survived. "Maybe coming here wasn't as safe as Saul thought." As the young girl and the older man on the tractor were approaching them, Rachel ran down to meet them.

"Where are we? What is our location?" The young girl and man were only about thirty meters from where Rachel and Joseph were standing.

As Rachel's shout echoed down the hillside, the man shut off the tractor and cupped his hands to his mouth, "You are in Ein Gev!"

15

The community of Ein Gev, known as a highly successful tourist village, is on the eastern shore of the Sea of Galilee. All that mattered to Joseph right then, however, was that it was solid ground. With cell phone in hand, Rachel was already relaying information of their whereabouts to whoever was on the other end of the call.

The older man who had come by tractor to their rescue was giving her details. He looked to be in his late fifties—maybe early sixties—and was dressed modestly in graying denim jeans supported by suspenders. His gray handlebar mustache looked as though it had not been trimmed in a couple of days. He'd taken off his plaid cap as he approached and shook Joseph's hand.

"Is this everybody? Are you all OK? I heard your plane overhead—the crash shook the entire village."

"I think we are. There were two others from the flight crew that made it out, they landed somewhere just up the mountain."

The old man followed Joseph's gesture and scanned the mountains. "Let's get you two down and inside. I'll get some people together to go and look for them; we know those mountains."

"We're fine, really." Joseph looked to Rachel for support, but her hand was blocking the ear that wasn't connected to her cell. "We can help."

Pointing toward the mountain behind where they stood, the man asked, "You see those cliffs up there? Those are the Arbel Cliffs. There are literally hundreds of caves scattered all along the ridges and valleys. I've been in those cliffs since I was a boy. I've probably been in every cave. Trust us, we know this land. Come down with us; I'll set some people out immediately and get the authorities on the phone."

Reluctantly, Joseph agreed and began following the tractor back down the hill.

The gentleman apologized—asking that his rudeness be forgiven—and introduced himself. "I am Maurice. Maurice Wachsmann."

"It's a pleasure to meet you. I'm Joseph Zeigler. The young lady talking on the cell phone over there is Rachel."

"Joseph it is. Well, you two have had quite an adventure, I must say that you landed in a good place. It was near here that Rabbi Jesus was believed to have healed the demon-possessed man, as described in the New Testament. Those cliffs are where the Sermon on the Mount took place. Are you familiar with this story?"

Joseph nodded. "I believe that there is a reference in each of the gospels of Matthew, Mark, and Luke."

"Ah, it is good to talk with someone familiar with the text," Maurice said, smiling. The old gentleman looked at

Joseph, chuckled, and said, "Well, you didn't fall out of the sky to listen to an old man reminisce now did you?"

Joseph noticed the young girl riding beside her grandfather and staring at him as they ground downhill.

"Hello, what is your name?" Startled, she looked at Joseph and then up at the old gentleman.

Smiling, Maurice reassured her, "It is OK, you can answer." The young girl did not speak. Finally, Maurice introduced her. "This is Kristina. She's a bit shy until she gets to know you."

"What was that rumbling sound? It scared our lambs."

Maurice laid a reassuring hand on her head. "Please, come down to our home. We can fix some nice hot tea and you can rest and freshen up if you would like." Rachel continued to talk on her phone but she walked along beside Joseph as he followed behind Maurice.

Finally, after ending her phone call, she briefed Joseph on who she was talking with. Rachel had, in fact, been talking with the king, who was in turn about to contact the IDF. They'd determined, based on the information she provided, that either a bomb was placed on the plane just prior to departure, or that there was a ground-to-air-missile fired.

"Do you think it is possible that it could have been Hamas?"

"Doubtful. There have not been any intelligence reports of Hamas in this area for some time now. But there's no real way of knowing who placed the bomb on board, and whether or not they did it knowingly or unwittingly, it could have been put in someone's luggage."

"Do you think it could have been the pilot or co-pilot?"

"Neither the king nor I think so. They would be difficult to pay off to risk their own lives, they are already paid very well by His Majesty, and more importantly, they went out of their way to save us. No, we need to focus on anyone who put luggage on the plane or had access during flight. I packed my luggage and don't remember any bombs," she said, her smile forced. ". . . which just leaves the flight crew who tried to save us, your luggage, and Hadashah the flight attendant."

"And Phillip." Rachel squinted at him against the sun. "Phillip both packed my bag and placed it on the plane; I never even got to see inside it."

"But he's had plenty of access to you alone, and to the king for that matter. That doesn't add up."

"Then the only person it could have been was Hadashah, and she got blown out the back of the plane with the explosion—perhaps not a master planner."

Just then, a gun shot sounded behind them. Joseph turned toward the sound, noting that Rachel had dropped to a half crouch and in one smooth movement had drawn a small automatic pistol from her waist band. It looked like a small model Glock, probably a nine millimeter. Just before Joseph had left the military they had started to transition over to the Glock. Joseph watched as a signal flare rose high above the village, showering red sparks as it landed about four hundred meters out in the Sea of Galilee. It was the crew of the plane signaling, trying to get their attention. In a moment, the Glock was tucked back into her waist band as Rachel turned back toward Maurice and his granddaughter with a smile.

Running back up the mountain was a bit different than going down. At least he was able to stay just ahead of Rachel as they met up with the crew. As Rachel and Joseph approached, the two men were already jogging down the mountain toward them. Their brilliant white and blue uniforms made them plainly visible against the rock. Joseph clasped each one in a handshake as Rachel embraced each one with a hug.

"Thank God," said the man, identified by his nametag as Captain K. Kelly. "We landed a few kilometers north, and pushed it to get to your position," he panted. The man stood to his full six feet and wiped sweat from his curled graying, black hair.

"Captain Kelly, I am Joseph, and this is Rachel. I'm so happy to see you. You did an incredible job getting us off that plane."

"It's just Keith, and I'm just glad we all made it." His southern accent was still harsh in the Hebrew language. He jerked a thumb at his partner who was panting off to the side. "This is Todd, Todd Lee."

The sun bounced off Todd's perfectly shaved head as he reached out to shake hands. "Oh baby! I can't believe we made it!" He looked just over six-feet tall and was thin as a rail. His wrinkles blended seamlessly into his smile lines, putting him somewhere between fifty and sixty.

"Gentlemen, I hate to break up the party but we need to get to Tiberias," advised Rachel. "Tiberias is just due west, across the sea, about ten kilometers away. A Sea Patrol boat has been instructed to stand by at Ein Gev Holiday Resort."

Maurice piped in, "It's just a short walk to the resort, and we will be passing by my house to get there. Do you have time for a bite to eat? And you should have something to drink before leaving." Joseph could tell he wasn't the only one whose throat was dry as he looked around their faces. The house was only five minutes away. As they entered, Maurice welcomed his guests to his *house of tzedakah*. He took off his cap and asked what they would like to drink.

Immediately Keith spoke up, "Sir, I would kill for some sweet ice tea."

Maurice stopped what he was doing, turned, and gave him a long look. "You're not Israeli, are you?"

Keith raised an eyebrow, "No sir, I am American."

"I can't believe it, of all the people to fall out of the sky, they have to send me somebody who wants ice tea. Young man, if you want iced tea, you'll have to wait until you get to the resort. *There* they have iced tea." As Maurice finished talking with Keith he glared at Todd and asked him what he would like to drink.

Todd glanced at Keith. "Some hot tea with lemon would be superb." Maurice laughed, and in a short time he had fixed everyone a delicious salami and cheese sandwich, complete with a kosher dill pickle and hot tea. Having finished using the bathroom, Rachel came back into the dining area followed closely by Kristina, who was beaming. Maurice looked up to find Rachel cradling his granddaughter's Ferret.

"Look Joseph, she looks just like Sweet Pea."

Maurice looked at the squirming fuzz ball. "Ah yes, my wife rescued her just before she passed away. She was in another village just beyond the mountain shopping when she noticed the little fur ball. There was a young boy in the market who had her for sale. Lydia fell in love with her immediately. Lydia. That was my wife." Joseph noticed that Maurice had tears in his eyes.

"That's a beautiful name," Joseph said.

"Yes, and she was a beautiful woman. I am sorry. You'll have to forgive an old man. I still get a little weepy when I think about her. It's been almost seven years since she passed. It's funny, but there's not a day that goes by that I don't think about her. We were both teenagers when we fell in love. Still, to this day, I don't know what she saw in me. But whatever it was I'm sure glad that she did. We sure had some good times together, and somehow along the way we managed to raise two great kids."

Joseph looked at Rachel's laughing face. Joseph smiled as he remembered the two of them chasing Sweet Pea all over Rachel's childhood home. They'd loved that little ferret. Sweet Pea loved nipping at Joseph's big sneakers. The two kids laughed when Sweet Pea would all but disappear into his empty shoes, and they'd cried as they buried Sweet Pea under the shade of a big tree in Rachel's backyard.

Kristina's little ferret was named Princess, but she could have been Sweet Pea's clone. Rachel hugged the little ball of sable fur before handing her to Joseph, who did not hesitate a second to do the same. Little Princess just clucked with excitement, her tail completely bottle-brushed.

Maurice invited everyone to sit down at a table and gave thanks for his granddaughter Kristina, for new friendships, and for great memories, past and future. Finally Maurice gave thanks for the food they were about to eat. As customary, Joseph and Rachel acknowledged Maurice's prayer with *"Le'chaim,"* Keith and Todd looked in his direction, puzzled.

"'To life,' gentlemen. *Le'chaim* is the Hebrew translation for the salutation 'to life.'"

Todd looked at Maurice. "What did you mean when you first welcomed us into your house of *tzedakah*?" Without pause Maurice told them that *tzedakah* is the Hebrew word for charity and that in Judaism, *tzedakah* referred to the religious obligation to perform charity, an important part of living a healthy spiritual life.

"You see Mr. Lee, there are many different types of charity. Some have greater meanings than others. For instance, when someone gives only when they are asked, that is one form. Giving when they are not asked is another. And giving anonymously is still another. In Judaism, giving anonymously is considered the second highest form of *tzedakah*."

"And the first?"

"Independence. Giving a person their independence is the highest form of charity. You see, when a person receives independence they do not have to depend on *tzedakah*, or any type of charity. Do you understand?"

Todd smiled. "Sir, independence is something I definitely understand."

As they were just about to finish eating, Rachel's cell phone began to beep. From her conversation Joseph surmised that the call was from the Sea Patrol. After assuring them that everything was all right, and telling the patrol that the group was en route, she gave a look that said they better hurry. As they rose to leave, Rachel, Todd, and Keith thanked Maurice for his hospitality, leaving only Joseph who reached out to shake the man's hand. He was surprised at the recognition in the man's hand, and apparently Maurice, too, was surprised at finding another Mason.

"Thank you, Achi, for all of your kindness." Maurice just smiled and bowed his head slightly. As Joseph turned to leave he noticed a small *pushkeh* attached to the wall with an old nail. Joseph slipped his hand into his pocket, removed a few coins, and dropped them into the small wooden poor box.

"May peace be unto you, Achi. Shalom."

Continuing to walk out the door, Joseph saw that Rachel, Todd, and Keith were already about a hundred meters up the road ahead of him, and he had to run to catch up. Joseph could see the patrol boat docking next to one of the piers. Just before he got on the gang plank Joseph glanced back toward Maurice's place. He could still see Maurice standing in his doorway, watching. Joseph raised his hand high in the air and waved. It was a good visit.

16

The patrol boat they boarded had a red hull and looked to be about twenty-six meters long; Joseph couldn't help but notice the fully manned twenty-millimeter stabilized cannon and machine gun on the foredeck. It looked as if Saul really wasn't taking any chances this time.

A car had been arranged for them once they made landfall, but currently it was nowhere in sight. Walking down the gang plank, Todd spotted a small restaurant that stuck out into the Sea of Galilee.

"Joseph, do you think that they speak English in there?"

"I should think so; all of the good tourist spots have staff that speaks it."

"Good. I'll be back in a couple minutes; I have an appointment with a cold beer." As Todd walked toward the restaurant, Keith and Joseph looked at each other, and quickly tagged along behind him. The restaurant was Decks' Gourmet Charcoal Grill and was surrounded by water on three sides. They found a seat by one of the railings.

Todd glanced at the menu. "Well Keith, they may not have iced tea, but they have Bud!"

Joseph laughed, nodding. "We do, and the drinks are on me. It's the least I can do for all you have done."

Grumbling, Keith ordered a Corona with lime. "I know you got sugar, and they have to have ice if they keep the beer cold, and this country is crazy about tea. What's it take to put the three together?"

"Make that *two* Coronas." Rachel dropped into the seat beside Joseph. "I contacted the driver, and there was a mistake with the address. We probably have time for a drink or two."

Each table had matching wooden flat-backed folding chairs. There was huge canopy of brown drapes that dropped from the center of the ceiling and tied to each side. High above there was a round wooden chandelier that was suspended from the center and lit the entire dining area. The floor looked as though it was made out of old recycled ship-decking, just like the railings on each of the three sides.

With just a few swallows remaining, Keith got to his feet, raised his beer, and offered a toast. "Here's to long-lasting friends—may our adventures continue, and may our feet always be planted firmly on the ground."

Todd stood. "And here's to His Majesty. He can make any man's life more interesting than he would care to have it." As they laughed and drank, Keith looked between Rachel and Joseph.

Keith leaned back in his chair. "We weren't sure if we should say anything until we were alone, but you really don't remember us do you, Joseph." Joseph stopped mid-swallow and put his beer down, throwing a look to Rachel as she was paying strict attention to her Corona's label. "Guess it's not really that surprising—you were still on some heavy meds when we made our exit."

"I'm not sure I'm following you."

Todd was running his hand over his head as he leaned in. "We first met Saul at a Masonic lodge near the Dhahran Air Field in Saudi Arabia. The king had been invited by the Masonic High Council of Egypt. We met out on a trail run and struck up a conversation. He's a fascinating guy, really is. Anyway, we kept in contact, and eventually, once our service contracts ran out, he hired us as security consultants and pilots. We first met when you were conked out in the hospital. Same as when we first met Rachel." Joseph looked questioningly at Rachel who was nodding her head at him.

Keith stepped in. "It was tough convincing that one to let us keep watch over you," he wagged a finger at Rachel, "but she needed to sleep sometime, to be ready for when Saul needed her. We excused ourselves when you came out of it, thought it was better for you to see familiar faces—yah know, better than having to look at Todd's egg head." Todd was smiling.

Joseph looked between the two men in disbelief, remembering how Rachel had hugged them when they had met off the mountain side. "I'm sorry I . . ."

Keith waved away the comment. "Hell, not many men live—let alone walk away—when a grenade goes off that close to 'em. We're just glad we got another chance to see you walkin' around again."

Joseph raised his glass, "To . . . to old friends, and new friends."

The car had arrived; Rachel pointed it out as it pulled against the curb. Finishing their drinks, the group pushed back their chairs and filed out. Joseph paid the bill and spotted Rachel approaching the yellow Mercedes shuttle. Keith and Todd met him midway. They both gave him a firm handshake and told him that they were to catch a taxi to Tel Aviv. Joseph waved good-bye one last time, saluting sharply.

Keith leaned across Todd as they got in the cab. "Hey, the next time I see you, I'll have you a cold glass of *real* sweet iced tea."

As Joseph watched their taxi round a curve, he felt a humbling spiritual presence in his midst. The world was full of brothers, and many were closer than he could know. Looking over at Rachel, Joseph saw she was still talking to the cabbie. As they made eye contact, she motioned for him to hurry.

17

As each summoned member of the Knesset arrived, they were shown to the palace's conference room, where Saul was waiting for them. Samuel worked his way around the room, offering wine and hors d'oeuvres consisting of white cheeses and melon slices. He'd rushed to fill in for Phillip, with whom he had been out of contact since he drove Joseph to the airport the previous day. The Knesset were joined by Special Forces personnel and gathered in the main conference area near the library. As everyone settled in, the king raised his hands for silence and turned the attention over to a large man in military fatigues.

Colonel Asaad was in his early sixties, but could have easily gone toe to toe with any man straight out of boot camp. "Gentleman, during the past ninety-six hours we have come across information that could threaten the stability of the state." The colonel allowed a few seconds for the collective members to push away their plates and wine glasses. "Four days ago, an attack on a close friend of the king, Joseph Zeigler, prompted us to look into those who might benefit from the king's removal. Please, don't look around, you would not have been summoned if you weren't above suspicion." A projector lit up the wall behind him showing the crash near Ein Gev. "The attackers have shown that they are capable of serious destruction in the pursuit of their goals, and Civil Aviation Authority determined that the explosion originated from inside the tail end of the plane. This meant that the explosive device had either been hand-carried onto the plane and placed in the rear, or it had been loaded into the cargo area underneath.

We can assume that there are some of the people whom we trust, whom the *king* trusts, who are, in reality, revolutionary operatives or sympathizers connected with this plot. What our opponent does not realize is how much information we have to work with. Evidence is piling up, and soon it will be enough to allow us to publicly denounce this traitor and put a stop to his plot. His Majesty, King Oman, would like your support in approving a plan that will not only locate the attackers at the compound, whose testimony may be the key to unveiling this traitor, but also may force our enemy to expose himself. Your Majesty."

As Colonel Asaad took his seat, Saul stood and moved to the podium. He held up a tattered and worn copy of the Bible. "This book was given to me many years ago by an evangelist visiting the country. I'm sure everyone here is familiar with the book of Matthew. Chapter twenty-six, verses fourteen through sixteen.

"Then one of the twelve, called Judas Iscariot, went unto the chief priests, and said unto them, What will ye give me, and I will deliver him unto you? And they covenanted with him for

thirty pieces of silver. And from that time he sought opportunity to betray him."

As the king closed the Bible he surveyed the faces before him. "I believe, like many of you, that a conspiracy has been going on for many years. The secret service has been accruing intelligence to suggest who is pulling the strings. However, without certain proof, I cannot remove this man without turning this monarchy, which my forefathers have built, into base despotism. I ask for your help, here, tonight my brothers, to approve my plan and help us remove this threat to our national security. Phase one, the locating of the burial site and the transfer of the body back to its rightful resting place, is within my authority; I have already put it into production. However, I will need to construct a small field headquarters and have use of several members of the ISF. These provisions are outlined in the folders that have been delivered to you.

We know who the Judas is. We also know that our Judas has enlisted the services of various individuals currently working at the new compound. And intelligence tells us that there are at least two other individuals with close ties to our Judas who have not, as yet, been identified: our bomber, and an agent who was seen following Joseph Ziegler. They are classified as *moles*. Phase two will be to lure these moles out into the open. Just like Judas Iscariot, these individuals will come to collect their thirty pieces of silver. Phase three will be to evoke a confession."

"Your Majesty," a young member of the Knesset, known to the king as Uri Miller, lifted the folder containing the provision above his head. "Your Majesty, I am most grateful for the trust you have placed in us. However, it is clear that you have invited the minimal personnel, and you are asking us to support a measure that is secretive in nature—in its passage, and vague in detail of its implementation."

Asaad gruffly cut him off before he could say more, "Let me remind our junior member that he is now in big boy school and playing by big boy rules. You better know how strong the limb is before you start walking out onto it." Several other members were chiding Miller as Saul raised his hands for silence.

"You may have been the only one to say it, but I'm sure that you were not the only one to think it. Mr. Miller is right, I have only asked for the minimal amount of persons necessary to approve this plan, the minimum necessary to oversee its completion. What I ask of you is trust, and if you give it to me, it is my belief that this threat, which has shadowed this government, will be resolved within thirty-six hours." Saul let the silence hang in the room for a moment. "All those in favor . . ." the members raised their hands in unison. Miller looked uncertainly at the king; as Saul looked back into his eyes, the king bowed slightly in respect. Uri shook his head before raising his hand as well.

The king raised his glass, "Here's to our nation, our Lord, and hopefully new friends." At this he nodded to Mr. Miller, "may the Supreme Architect of the Universe delight to dwell with and bless each of us. Shalom."

The meeting concluded quickly, each member being sworn to secrecy—with their approval—until the conclusion of the proposal. Being the last to leave, and seeing that he was alone with the king, Colonel Asaad approached. "Is there anything that I can personally do to assist with the operation?"

"Actually, there is. I would greatly appreciate it if you will personally oversee it." Colonel Asaad made a quick bow of assertion, acknowledging the confidence that the king had shown him, and extended his right hand. The king responded in like manner, and the two whispered to each other before parting. The colonel, taking a step back, placed his right hand over his heart, bowed at the waist, and left the room. It had been a good meeting, and the king was pleased that so much had been accomplished. It was now time to implement the plan, leak the information, and to see how long it would be for those involved to return for their spoils.

18

Rachel and Joseph made the sixty-five-kilometer trip from Tiberias to Haifa in just under an hour. Their conversation en route was limited, even as the driver rambled on about whatever apparently random thought floated through his head.

As the taxi pulled into the entryway of Le Meridien Hotel, Joseph and Rachel made their escape, tossed the fare into the man's outstretched hand, and made their way directly into the hotel. Rachel laughed and whispered in Joseph's ear, "Saul can't even manage to hide someone without opulence."

The clerks were clones of one another, except for the gender differences. Their midnight navy suits were crisp and professional as they stood erect behind the hotel's highly polished desks. Plate glass windows overlooked the Mediterranean Sea in a lobby decorated with rich leather furniture. A huge chandelier showered fractured light over them as they approached a male attendant

behind the check-in desk. His golden nametag flashed—
Abe.

Rachel sighed as she took it all in, and she watched
Joseph as he gave the name they'd been given by Saul and
was handed room keys. Joseph caught her demure smile
before she turned quickly away and walked toward the café.
She had always loved to travel when they were growing
up. Tucking the room keys into his pocket, Joseph followed
her and found her seated at a table, watching the sailboats
and yachts pass in the distance past a plate glass window. A
waiter was just leaving the table as Joseph arrived.

"I ordered you a dessert, and a Turkish coffee."

Joseph smiled at her as he sat down. She knew he had
always loved coffee, even as a child; Rachel's mother had
quickly labeled him as the Royal Bean Taster. "There is a
mistake with our reservations; there's only one room."

Rachel looked at him and smiled. "No mistake, the
room is large and it's all we need. The waiter returned in
less than a minute and served the coffee in bone china cups
with saucers. The cake was served on matching dessert
plates. Rachel dug right in. "I just realized how hungry I am,
my god, we'll have to eat again soon. After all, there's not
too much you can do lying low. I'm going to get a shower as
soon as we get in the room, and we need to get to the stores
before they close. Our luggage is probably still smoldering
somewhere in Ein Gev."

In a few minutes, Rachel and Joseph were making
their way to their luxurious suite. The suite overlooked
the sea. Rachel excused herself and entered what was more
a spa than a bathroom. The glass-enclosed steam shower
beckoned her.

The steamy water pounded and massaged every pore of her body, and it was difficult to find the will to drag herself out. She donned the plush white terry cloth robe that lay draped across the vanity stool and wrapped a towel around her hair before walking barefoot back into the living room, where Joseph had poured her a glass of wine.

"Chianti, still your favorite right?" She nodded as she took the glass. "I'd like to accompany you shopping, maybe get some 'personal shopper' advice?" She nodded, sipping her wine as he vanished into the bathroom.

Lying on the bed Rachel felt the soft cotton and luxuriated in the view of the ocean. In a surprisingly short time, Joseph appeared. He was still wet from the shower and was also sporting a monogrammed robe. Laughing, she pulled the towel from around her head and flung it over his, running her hands through his hair. As Joseph managed to catch her hands and pull the towel free, he found himself staring into her eyes, her hands within his.

Slowly the smile left Rachel's face. She leaned toward him, her hands rose to his chest, and she kissed him. Joseph felt her soft lips on his as water slowly trickled down his face and ran around the corner of her lips. Slowly, he released her hands and wrapped his own around her waist, pulling her against him. As he returned her kiss, she could feel his strength behind it; she closed her eyes as his grip tightened around her. *Is this really happening?* Rachel pulled her hands up to his face and stroked the angles of his jaw, feeling the rasp of his stubble as it tingled against her palm. *Was she really here, in this beautiful hotel, with the arms of the only man she had ever loved around her, pulling her closer against him?* She felt his hands pull away the sash that tied her robe, and she quickly did the same to his, guiding him toward the bed. As their bodies became entwined under the cool sheets, Rachel hid her face in his shoulders to conceal her smile as she thanked God for giving her the love of her life.

The Chianti had been given ample time to breathe before they drank it. Without a word they re-showered, this time together. Twenty minutes later, they disembarked in a taxi heading toward Simcha Golan Way and walked into the Grand Canyon Mall, the largest shopping area in Haifa. The crowds were bustling.

Rachel and Joseph each bought a weeks' worth of shirts, pants, and underwear, paying with the black card. Joseph walked away with a few polos and an alligator belt picked by Rachel, while she in turn splurged on makeup and, of course, lilac perfume. All the while, Rachel couldn't help but hold Joseph's hand; he pulled her close to his side as they made their way from shop to shop.

Famished, they headed back to the hotel and into the restaurant for filet mignon and Caesar salad, paired with another bottle of Chianti. Haifa was almost a dream, and Rachel and Joseph spent the next three days walking on the beach and through the streets shopping and sightseeing, all the while reminiscing about their childhood. Some days they barely made it out of the room, trying to make up for all the years that had been lost between them.

One night, as he held Rachel tightly and stroked her arm, Joseph spoke softly to her, "I think I remembered something—something from our childhood." Rachel sat up and looked at him, waiting for him to go on. "Why haven't you ever married?" Rachel just looked at him, confusion on her face as she pulled the covers back up over her. "When we were children, I remember us outside a cave, playing, and you talking to me in French, calling me your love. I think we were more than just childhood crushes; I think we were together. Sometimes I get these feelings when I see you, like I'm remembering emotions without images. But I lost all that, Rachel, I really did. I lost it. I became a new person, one who barely knew you."

Rachel had tears in her eyes as she looked at him. "When your doctor said it was just temporary, I had so much hope. But, as time went on, I realized that you might never remember; I know you still don't. But, I don't expect you to remember, and I don't care if you remember, because I do, and you are still the same person as you were before. Your commander should have known that Shamir was too strong. You sacrificed so much, but you saved so many. I sat by you every day for three weeks, wondering if you were going to wake up. If you hadn't had your body armor you probably would have never made it to the hospital. I knew that if you didn't remember who I was, I would just have to get you to know me again, because I wasn't going to lose you."

He pulled Rachel close to him and they held each other in silence before Joseph finally broke in, "Rachel, I love you. I've felt this way as long as I can remember, and beyond that. Whenever I remember you, you're smiling, and I feel a happiness I can't explain. I'm sorry I've taken so long. I don't know if I'll ever remember, but I know you here and now, and I love you with all that I am."

She was crying as she smiled. She laughed as she grabbed Joseph around the neck and clung to him. "I love you too! I have always loved you and I have never stopped loving you, not for a single moment, not even once, not ever. Do you understand?" With a kiss, they fell back onto the covers, and into the embrace of the night.

Joseph didn't know what time it was when he awoke, but he could tell that it was late because daylight trickled in through the windows. He checked the clock sitting on the bedside table—eight twenty-two. He couldn't remember when he had gotten such a good night's sleep. Rising up to check his surroundings, he found Rachel still asleep next to him. He was careful not to wake her as he carefully slunk to the bathroom and splashed water on his face. He watched the water as it drained away and thought about Rachel, and his fortune, *Or was it fate?* It was as though an angel had once again whispered in his ear, and he tried to process it. Was this fortuitous, or was it fate? The attack had changed the path of his life. Everything that had happened—every single thing that had occurred—had led up to this point. He and Rachel were together again, and it seemed curiously natural. From the bedroom he could hear Rachel calling for him.

"I am here, *mon chéri.*" Hearing the words come out of his mouth, Joseph quickly looked up and stared at his own reflection in the mirror. *Where did that come from?* he thought. He was not accustomed to talking like this. *Who in the hell is this man?* He smiled and wondered what kind of spell he was under. Rachel threw back the covers, got up out of bed, and found Joseph in the lavatory, leaning on the sink basin. He turned toward her as she entered.

As Rachel stood in the doorway, the light from the bedroom window was shining off her form—she looked like an angel. Her body was shaped with fine lines and smooth curves, and Joseph could just stare at her sleek figure. "You look amazing."

Joseph walked over to Rachel, reached down, picked her up, and carried her back into the bedroom. He placed her on the bed and then lay down beside her, tucking her in to the covers.

He told her for the first time what had happened to him during the conflict with the Palestinians. He told her that the reason he treasured the few memories he had of Rachel and Saul was that most of the memories he got back were of the horrors of war. He could not erase the sight and smell of the dead and the pain of loss.

Rachel took his hand, assuring him, "I am with you now and everything will work out. Together we will be OK." Rachel understood only too well the dilemma that Joseph was facing. She had been there many times while working as a special op with the IDF's Sayeret Matkal.

"Sometimes I wonder if these two people I remember can even be the same person. As a child, I saw things so differently than I do now."

"We were both children, and I can say the same thing," she told him, "The world is never as children imagine it will be. It is always harder, and more beautiful than we can ever think. The important thing is to appreciate each equally. The fact that we have found each other again is amazing and beautiful to me, Joseph, and now all we have to do is just love one another."

19

The sun was scorching as Paul sat atop the struts of the temple, going over a few welding seams. Business had gone on as usual after the overseer's disappearance. A few new guys had been brought in to help get them past the setbacks caused by the confusion, and a substitute had moved into the main office. *No, substitute makes it sound like it's temporary. A replacement.* Paul frowned as he looked down; he could pick out Hazar over the scaffolding's drop-off, chatting with one of the new workers. What was worse was that they had never even seen a cent of the money they were owed. They'd been told that they had failed. *Failed!* They had put a body in the ground, they had killed the man, and they had that stain upon their souls.

"What do you mean *reward?*" Hazar put his level down as he looked at the temp who had just unloaded a wheelbarrow of stone next to him.

The worker wiped his brow with a handkerchief from his pocket. "Like I said, they're offering a reward for information, and a much bigger reward for a necklace the guy was wearing. But, don't even think about buying any ol' chain; my buddy was just about arrested for trying to pawn off some shoddy piece for the money. Guess it was something special; they know just what they're looking for. But, like I said, information gets you something if it helps the investigation."

As the man walked away and back toward the stone cutting, Hazar's mind was working fast. *Had there been a necklace?* He looked around for Andrew and found him setting a frame. "Andrew! Come here, where's Paul?"

The frame settled in position, and workers began securing it into place. "What's wrong Hazar? You look spooked." As Hazar motioned him away, Andrew handed his portion off to a fellow worker, and the two made their way to the lunch tables.

"Brother, we have a chance to earn back the money we lost." Andrew looked around and leaned in closer. "One of the new workers, he told me the king has offered a reward for information, and even more for the return of a necklace he was wearing."

Andrew looked at his brother and smiled. "And the necklace, you have it?"

Hazar looked sheepishly at his brother. "I was hoping you might have taken it." The two turned and looked up toward Paul, who waved down at them. "Paul then?"

"He must have, but he would have given it to us, surely; he isn't stupid enough to try to hide it." Hazar tried not to think about the Rolex he had carried in his pocket since the day they had attacked the overseer. God only knew what would happen if Andrew knew he had been holding out. Andrew waved Paul over. Paul glanced at the time and began his climb down the scaffolding.

"What if he doesn't have it?" Hazar looked questioningly at his brother. "What if we missed it, and it's buried?"

Andrew squinted. "Then we dig it up."

"I'm not sure getting close to the . . . hill . . . again would be a good idea."

"You don't have the capacity in your brain to process any of the thoughts that you have. You just need to keep your thoughts to yourself." Hazar tried to rise from his seat, but Andrew's hand was on his shoulder in a second, squeezing. Trying not to yell out, Hazar was forced again into a sitting position, but Andrew didn't let up. "This whole thing was a mistake Hazar—every second of it—and we need to get ourselves out of it. You will listen to me, Hazar." He released his grip, and Hazar shied away, rubbing his neck, as Paul arrived.

"What is it, brothers?" The two looked at him, and their moods soured.

Andrew indicated for Paul to sit beside Hazar. "Did you take anything from the other night?"

Paul looked between the two. "You mean *the night?* No, what would I take?"

Andrew sat back and crossed his arms. "That settles it—we go back tonight."

Paul looked at Andrew, and then at Hazar. "Go back where?"

"Yes, it's them." About ninety meters away, the worker who had talked with Hazar was on a cell phone, watching the group. "I watched the parking lot this morning; they drove a sixty-three Dodge, beat-up truck. I told one of them about the reward and they're already meeting."

On the other end of the phone line, Ben-Zur tapped a pencil on his desk. "All right, I'm on my way; go ahead and move to phase two." Grabbing his coat and chuckling to himself, he was out the door. It was only a twenty-minute drive to the site. The king had asked him to find and detain the suspects until requested. Circumstantial evidence wasn't enough to hold the brothers, but the inspector borrowed an idea from one of his favorite books, the Book of Genesis. The scriptures tell that Joseph tested his brothers and had one of his stewards put his silver cup in Benjamin's sack cloth with his corn money. Taking from this story, the inspector had one of the undercover field agents working at the compound.

As the workers completed another day's work, they all gathered together in the main yard. The inspector stepped up onto one of the work tables, and the din of the site quickly quieted as they noted the uniformed men filing in.

"All right, listen up." Lifting his arms above his head, he waved the general grumbling into quiet. "I was called here because the new overseer has informed me that the blueprints for the temple were stolen, sometime between this morning and afternoon. As standard procedure, each worker must open any personal containers and empty their pockets for inspection as they leave the yard."

Hazar felt his face blanche as he clutched the watch in his pocket. Police patrolled the sides of the line, and Hazar felt sweat on his forehead as they approached the inspector. He waited, watching the guards, hoping for a moment to toss the watch without anyone seeing. It was hopeless;

there were too many people, and then it was too late. Hazar stepped up to the inspector, and turned out his pockets. The inspector immediately snatched up the watch and glared at the workman. "And where by chance does someone like you get a watch like this?"

Hazar controlled his breathing but couldn't match the man's eyes. "It was a gift, Inspector."

Hazar watched in horror as a thin smile crawled across the man's face; he knew that Andrew too was watching with burning eyes. "Well," the inspector began, "you might want to find better friends. This cheap imitation wouldn't fool my daughter! You can tell by the numbers, all wrong." The inspector all but threw the watch back to Hazar and waved him on. "Keep it moving!" Hazar scrambled forward. *It isn't a fake! It's impossible, isn't it? Was it luck?* He was not going to question the inspector's decision. Hazar slid the watch back into his pocket and moved past the gate.

Paul was in line ahead of Andrew; he opened his backpack and allowed them to inspect it. The inspector raised an eyebrow and tapped the lunch pail he carried for the three of them. As Paul opened the lunch box he could not believe his eyes. Folded neatly within were the blueprints for the temple. Without thinking, Paul reached in and picked them up, staring dumbfounded at his brothers.

Hazar immediately spoke up, "There has been a terrible mistake. Our brother would never take the blueprints—there's been some sort of mistake!"

"That's something we can sort out in detention." The inspector grabbed the wide-eyed Paul and signaled to his men. "You two are his brothers, yes? We'll have to take you in for questioning as well." Enraged, Andrew flung himself at Paul and struck him with one fierce blow after another, forcing the inspector to step back and out of range. One of the officers moved to gain control and dug a taser into Andrew's back, bringing the man to his knees. Paul collapsed beside him, leaving Hazar to look on, dumbfounded. Each was quickly handcuffed and whisked away to the main detention facility downtown.

The inspector pulled out his cell and dialed the king. "We have them, Your Majesty."

"You're sure?" Saul stood from his desk.

"Three men, brothers, one very large, driving a beat-up Dodge truck, and with the Rolex—as per your description—on their person."

"Did you let him keep it, Inspector?"

"Yes, Your Majesty. Just as you have advised, they have no reason to think they are under suspicion for anything more than theft. But, Your Majesty, surely we could work a confession from them at this point—"

"If we wanted to lose the bigger fish I would say yes, but we still need more—we need a confession from our Judas if we are to put him away." The king sat back in his chair. "When the stage is set, we will release our actors."

20

After the fifth ring Joseph answered the cell phone. It'd been set to vibrate and had been scooting across the nightstand, evading his groggy hands.

"Hello, Joseph, how are you doing?" Joseph immediately recognized the king's voice and turned on the bedside light. He looked to his right and discovered that Rachel was not in bed. The lavatory light was on, and he could tell that Rachel was moving about.

"Your Majesty, I had not expected to hear from you so soon."

"Joseph, phase two will be taking place sooner than we had expected."

"Phase two, Your Majesty?"

"Yes Joseph, we're ahead of schedule. We believe tonight the three individuals who attacked you will be headed back to get the jewel."

"Are we ready for phase two, Your Majesty? I mean, it's only been six days. What could you have possibly gotten accomplished in six days?"

"Don't forget, Joseph," replied the king, "in six days God created the Heavens and the Earth. Rachel will fill in the blanks during your flight. There will be a helicopter sitting on your roof within the next half hour. You need to be on it. I'll see you at low twelve." Joseph looked to see what time it was. The bedside clock indicated that it was nine forty-five. Rachel emerged from the bath fully dressed in black camouflage pants, vest, and combat boots. She walked over to where Joseph was sitting on the bed, leaned down, gave him a couple of kisses on his lips, and informed him that they only had eight or nine minutes to get upstairs if they were going to meet the king at midnight.

"Why am I always the last one to get told about things?" he said, slipping past her and finding clothes to throw on. You look great by the way—where did you get the outfit?"

Rachel smiled. "Remember, I am a very self-reliant girl! There's one in the bathroom for you too; Saul had them delivered." Within a few minutes, Joseph had managed to get up and get ready. Fortunately, Rachel had already packed his clothes with hers and had their belongings up on the helipad. As they climbed the flight of stairs to the roof, the helicopter was on its final approach. The plane touched down softly, and Rachel and Joseph boarded what Joseph recognized as a Special Forces helicopter nicknamed "The Panther"—the shrouded tail rotor gave it away. The crew wasted no time in lifting off and heading toward their final destination as the two strapped in.

Their rendezvous point was only about eighty-three kilometers from Le Meridien. With a cruising speed around one hundred fifty knots, it would only take about fifteen to twenty minutes before touchdown. They departed from

Haifa and traveled south, parallel along the Armistice line toward Budrus. As they approached the western edge of Samaria they would turn southwest toward the Shomron Mountains. Once on the ground, they would meet with Colonel Asaad and receive their final instructions. Approaching the landing area from the north side, the Panther touched down about a hundred meters from the crest of the hill. Rachel and Joseph waited until the rotors had come to a stop before they slid the side door back and stepped out. The air was crisp, a little cooler than Haifa. Barely a sliver of moon hung above their heads. They could see headlights here and there, and it was one of these that they approached.

Walking from the landing zone, Rachel and Joseph found Colonel Asaad briefing several other members of the reconnaissance team with the latest intelligence. They caught the end of it as he gave the current movements of the three brothers using maps of satellite images that he had laid out on the hood of his jeep. Rachel approached about three paces behind the colonel and made her presence known. As the colonel turned, Rachel clicked her heels together and came to attention. The colonel immediately looked at Joseph and back at Rachel.

He locked eyes with Joseph. "Good, Miss Barack will accompany you into the underground; we've set up a cramped but functioning command center within the hillock." He turned to Rachel and said, "Give him his final briefing and get prepared; we have only fifteen minutes from when the truck passes our lookout to be ready."

Another salute and an about-face, and Commander Rachel Barack quickly turned and walked away. Rachel's military rank was junior officer or "seren," which was the same as a captain. Colonel Asaad's rank was senior officer, or brigade commander. Rachel was only two ranks below Colonel Asaad; however, those two ranks were thought to be more difficult to obtain than picking a winning lottery number. At a security checkpoint leading into the main portion of the underground chamber, Rachel and Joseph were met by another member of Colonel Asaad's special unit and were escorted inside. The entrance was barely two feet wide, undetectable once a thick earthen flap was lowered. This flap was pulled back so that Rachel and Joseph could enter, single file.

"Joseph, directly above us should be the grave—your grave." Rachel smirked as they walked, half crouched, through the small tunnel that brought them deeper into the hillock. It was hastily constructed, but the engineers had shored up the walkway well, and it opened into a six-by-six-foot area with clearance to the top of the hill. A coffin sat on a small hydraulic lift. Joseph looked uncomfortably at Rachel. "Once Saul had this location he immediately started working. He met with members of the Knesset, who approved the use of the ISF, and ISS and construction.

Information was then leaked to the workers at the compound that you were missing, and a reward was offered for the return of the jewel. The IDF immediately began to receive bits and pieces of information from the workers who were interested in the reward money. Field agents were placed to monitor the workers, and their intelligence led us to three brothers. We also received information that indicates that Phillip is somehow involved.

We're not sure how deeply as of yet, but our little stint in Ein Gev is certainly looking more and more suspicious.

We'll be set up in a small command post just beyond the brush line, and the area has been set up with cameras to keep us informed on how you are doing."

Joseph had climbed the small stepladder and was now inspecting the box. "I take it I won't be lying cozy with the rest of you in the command post," he said. On the lift—a scissor raiser, like a cherry picker—was a bolted down coffin, painted black and outfitted with hidden handrails. There were a dozen or so floodlights attached to the base, at least six lights on each side. Alternately hidden between the floodlights were small hoses that were connected to compressed $CO2$ canisters located beneath. Once the floodlights were turned on, the smoke would be released. "At least there isn't a lid to nail down over me."

Rachel set her hands on her hips. "Joseph, I won't be in the command post either; I'll be watching over you, along with several others. Colonel Asaad should be in shortly to brief you on the final details." Although he had not been formally briefed, Joseph had an idea as to what his mission was going to be. The inside of the box was large enough for an adult to lie down in without any dis-comfort. Just to the right of the lift, hanging on the wall, was a set of clothing and a pair of sandals, which Rachel advised Joseph that he needed to put on. Joseph quickly removed his outer garments and put on the clothing as Rachel watched.

"Why is it that I always seem to be taking my clothes off when I'm with you now, Rachel?"

She laughed, "I'm just lucky I guess."

"Ah, flak jacket, well now I feel safe." Rachel just shook her head at the sarcasm.

As Joseph finished lacing up the sandals, he continued his examination of the chamber. Looking above the lift, toward the top of the chamber, he noticed what looked like a mine shaft attached to the chamber's ceiling, extending down. He scaled the ladder and lay down in the box and looked up the shoot that extended all the way up to the top of the hill, ending in a wall of earth. Rachel was leaning up against the lift when she heard someone coming through the tunnel.

As he stood to his full height, the colonel looked at Rachel. "How is he doing?" With a nod of her head, Rachel directed the colonel's attention toward the lift. "Ah, Mr. Ziegler, how are you? I see that you're in the box; don't worry, that's just a grass pallet at the top. The lift will press the box right through."

"I'm all right, though I'm not sure what all right means sitting in your own coffin."

"Everything is set on our end; it'll be fine. The king assured me that you would be up to the challenge."

"What do you mean, Colonel?"

"I had . . . reservations about using someone who hasn't had a covert ops mission in years, but the king informed me that you had plenty of experience in subterfuge. You know what the box is for—are you ready? Because if you aren't I need to know pretty damn soon."

Joseph rose from the box and looked Asaad in the eye. "Colonel, are you familiar with the Book of Genesis, the fiftieth chapter, and the twenty-sixth verse?" The colonel raised an eyebrow and shook his head. Joseph dropped to ground level and walked toward the man. "Well, let me see if I can help. Verse twenty-six says, 'So Joseph died, being a hundred and ten years old, and they embalmed him, and he was put in a coffin in Egypt.' Yes Colonel, I understand my role here."

The colonel nodded. "I'm sorry I questioned it, sir." Colonel Asaad placed his hand on Joseph's shoulder, and in doing so they both turned toward the box. "We'll be in constant communication," Asaad said, handing Joseph a tiny earpiece and helping him fit it. "Once you break the surface, you'll be blinded momentarily by the lights, so let it adjust. Commander Barack will be the voice in your ear since you've been in contact for the last week or so." The colonel handed her a mic that she fit, smiling at Joseph. "She'll be keeping you informed of *everything* that you can't see, including the targets' approach and when your part in the operation will commence.

If everything works accordingly, the three should be blinded by the floodlights and think that Joseph's spirit once again walks the earth. By then the smoke should be rolling over the hill and—," The colonel pulled out a small skin-toned disk and stuck it to Joseph's neck. "This is a mini microphone; we set up speakers around the area, and your voice will be echo-casted over the hillside." The colonel was smiling. "When you confront these traitors, we need a confession—a full confession: who they work for, why they did it, how much they were paid. All of this will be carefully monitored from the main communications post, and their movements will be closely monitored via seven different video cameras that have been set up and concealed around the top of the hill. Any threat to you will result in immediate neutralization by one of three sharpshooters."

The colonel reached into his jacket pocket. "One last thing Joseph, here is your jewel. The jewel of the junior grand warden. I knew that you would want it back." The colonel placed the jewel around Joseph's neck and then slipped it underneath his flak jacket.

Having concluded his briefing, Colonel Asaad extended his right hand. Joseph extended his; they shook, each recognizing the other's familiar grip.

"*Behatzlacha*, Achi."

"And good luck to you, colonel. *Shalom*, Achi."

The colonel left, and the two were left in the small space. Rachel grabbed Joseph's hand and pulled him into a kiss. For a moment they just stood together, resting their foreheads against each other, before a voice crackled into Joseph's ear that movement had been detected along the path leading to the brow of the hill. Rachel heard it too, and glancing into his eyes, she darted back out the entrance. As she made her way out, she flipped her mic's channel. "Joseph, can you hear me?"

Joseph picked up the walkie-talkie; he wouldn't have it once things got rolling. "I can hear you, Rachel."

"Good, I'm on my way to my overlook. The brothers have been spotted. I'll keep you informed, out."

The brothers had finally been released from detention, and it had taken them all evening to retrieve their rusted-out Dodge from the city lot where it had been impounded. The travel back to the *Sanctum Sanctorum* was fraught with chatter between Paul and Hazar as they questioned how close they had come to the law and wondered how

The Chamber of Truth

the blueprints had gotten in Paul's possession. Even more alarming was the sudden, unexplained release.

Andrew had snatched the release papers from Paul's hands, eliciting a laugh from Paul. "Andrew, you know you can't read. Let me see it." This earned him a bloody lip, but he got the papers back. It seemed like a trap, yet no one was following them. No one could suspect their deed, or they would still be locked up. Of course, Andrew had pawned the Rolex as soon as they had gotten out. He'd tackled Hazar and gotten in a few good hits before taking the watch and dropping it at the first shop they came to. The broker at Seted bought it for a pittance; just as the inspector had said, it was a fake.

The shopkeeper had looked it over and then looked up at the brothers. "It's a pretty poor imitation actually, but I think I might be able to find a buyer for it. Rivee, come take this to the back and see what we can do with it." He smiled as the brothers left, and the money went straight into getting the truck back. While his brothers argued their theories back and forth, Andrew remained quiet. All he could focus on was finding the jewel.

Arriving at the foot of the hill, the three brothers got out of the truck and began to hike the trail that led to the brow.

Joseph's heart raced. It had been a long time since he had worked in special ops. It had been even longer since he had worked a covert operation. And this was definitely a covert operation. His only solace was Rachel, continuing to reassure him in his ear.

As Rachel watched, the three individuals begin to climb up the hill through the scope of her rifle. The brothers were not wasting any time in their attempt to retrieve the jewel. Hazar was carrying an oil lantern in front leading the way with Andrew following. Paul was carrying another lantern and bringing up the rear. Surveillance could pick up every word the brothers uttered. "This is a bad idea, Andrew," Hazar said, looking around nervously. He could see nothing past the small circle of light from the lantern.

Andrew glared at his brother over his shoulder. "Let me remind you what happened the last time you thought it necessary to give your opinion, Hazar."

Hazar kicked the back of Andrew's leg and caused the man to tumble forward, barely managing to hold the lamp upright. Andrew jerked around and grabbed his brother by the collar.

Hazar managed to break from his brother's hold and stood, his hands balled into fists. "I'm not afraid of you, Andrew. The apron strings have been cut for a long time now. I'm ready. Come on."

Staring at Hazar, Andrew pulled up his tunic and slid his hand inside his waistband. He pulled his hand back out; his thumb and forefinger were pointed like a kid pretending to have a gun. Slowly he let his hand drop back to his side.

Turning, he faced Paul. "Well, after all these years, your brother finally has the balls to stand up for himself. When is it going to be your time?" Paul just looked at the ground. "Just as I expected." He turned and continued walking up toward the brow of the hill.

"You're gonna get us all killed! It's a trick Andrew—if we give them the jewel they will say we killed him. If they believe it, they will find the truth!" Andrew didn't listen as his lamp light fell on the sprig of acacia. Seeing the fear in Paul's eyes, Hazar snorted in anger and turned back to help his brothers dig. "Paul, our brother has lost his mind."

21

As she watched the three brothers approach, Rachel whispered through the earpiece to let Joseph know that the time had come. Beneath him, Joseph felt the machinery come to life. As Andrew lifted his shovel to break the earth, the hydraulic lift was activated. In one swift motion the lift raised Joseph into place, and his box accelerated toward the thin earthen covering. When they heard the hydraulic movements beneath the surface, the three stopped in unison and took a step back from the grave. As they did, the coffin burst from the surface, and dirt and stone rolled toward their feet. Right then the floodlights were freed from the darkness and brilliantly illuminated the sky. Rays of light sprang in every direction, turning the dark night to day, and the three brothers dropped to the ground, covering their heads. Smoke poured down the hillside, enveloping the brothers in a blanket. Paul dropped down to pray. Andrew cursed, waving at the smoke around him and trying to get a clear image of what was going on. Suddenly, the brothers saw the shadowy figure of a man rise up out from the cloud of smoke, climbing out from the earthen grave.

Just as Joseph stood, the floodlights were cut off, and the smoke began to settle around the top of the hill. Now, with only the small lanterns to provide light for them, the three brothers recognized Joseph standing at the foot of the grave.

Paul began shaking where he knelt on the ground reciting a forgiveness benediction; he rocked back and forth, his eyes wide and staring. "Forgive us Father, for we have sinned. Pardon us, our King, for we have transgressed. For Thou art a pardoner and a forgiver. Blessed art Thou, Lord, Gracious One who forgives abundantly." As Paul continued to recite the benediction he looked over to his brother Hazar.

Hazar had a look of sheer shock and bewilderment on his face. He looked upon the face of death itself as it stared back at him. He was filled with a fear that he had never experienced. It was uncontrollable and paralyzing, painful as it squeezed his organs into a pit. He wasn't even aware he'd lost control of his bladder. All the bad and evil he had ever done was now upon him, and all he wanted was one more day to prove that he was not a horrid creature. Hazar managed to turn his gaze on Andrew, and Andrew could see the panic and confusion in Hazar's eyes. He knew how afraid his brother was.

Andrew looked deep into Hazar's eyes and pulled him close, saying, "Hazar, you were right. My selfishness has caused this. I fear the army of Adonai is upon us. *Ani Mitzta'er, Achi!*" Trying to let his brother know he was sorry, Andrew knew that, deep within the secret recesses of his heart, everything that was happening was because of him. He knew that it was greed that had brought him to this point. It was well past midnight, and the cool night air gave a crisp new feel as one day shifted into another.

Temporarily blinded by the floodlights as he was lifted up through the burial portal, Joseph listened as Rachel whispered direction and guidance through the earpiece. "They are cowering, Joseph, eleven o'clock." Following Rachel's direction, Joseph turned toward where Andrew was now kneeling. Communication from other spotters in the field was continually being dispatched to Rachel. From this, she could sort and relay information to Joseph about what was taking place in every shadow of the night. From the very start, Colonel Asaad made it very clear that there was absolutely no room for error. So far, everything was going according to plan.

Joseph's eyes were finally adjusting to the darkness with the assistance of the lanterns that the brothers had brought with them. Joseph decided that it was time to begin. Keeping his head down, he slowly began to move forward, away from the grave, and toward Andrew.

As the spirit was moving relentlessly toward him— the one who had been his murderer—Andrew began to shake and move backwards on his knees. *"He's moving back slightly, he's very scared, he—"* In a flash, Andrew's hand dived into his tunic. A handgun flashed and pointed, and two shots rolled out, pounding Joseph in the chest. The men were less than five meters away from each other. Rachel felt tears forming in her eyes that she fought to keep down. *He's wearing a flak jacket—oh God please let him be OK.* The impact of the bullets resounded around the site; the blast was picked up by the small microphone on his collarbone.

No one moved. Andrew's movements had taken everyone by surprise; even the sharpshooters who had their sights fixed on the trio. Silence hung in every corner of resurrection hill. Rachel watched from her spotter's post overlooking the brow; she did not allow herself to run to him. She watched the entire episode unfold before her— Joseph was still standing. Her scope hovered over his statue-like form. He did not move, react, or respond in any way.

Colonel Asaad stared at his monitor for a second longer; the communications were silent. "Report!"

In a wave the IDF sharpshooters' voices were every-where as they asked for direction. "Shot's fired! Shot's . . ."

". . . Permission to . . ."

". . . fired! Awaiting . . ."

". . . Colonel, do we hold . . . ?"

Communication inquiries were coming at once, overlapping and garbling the messages. The sharpshooters had regained their focus, and Rachel knew their fingers were resting on the triggers, ready to squeeze.

Colonel Asaad overrode the communications, "All units, stand by and maintain radio silence."

Rachel switched back to her secure frequency with Joseph. "If you're OK, let me know by slightly raising your chin."

Joseph immediately raised his chin. Rachel took her first breath since the shots had rung out. Rachel could see what looked like two small bullet holes that had perforated just below the neckline of Joseph's robe. Once again Rachel whispered into Joseph's earpiece, "Joseph, if you wish to continue with the operation, then raise your chin and look straight ahead." Joseph complied and leveled his chin.

Rachel immediately switched back to her broad channel, "The operation is still a go."

In turn Colonel Asaad radioed his field units and instructed them to continue to stand by. As Joseph slowly raised his chin, he realized that he was staring into the face of someone he hadn't seen in over twenty years. He did not want to believe it, but his eyes told him it was true. Joseph stood looking at his old friend for several moments as memories swam through his head.

"What is your name?" Joseph had forgotten that the small microphone was still on. His voice resonated across the hillside.

Andrew let the pistol fall from his hands, as Joseph's gaze fell upon him. "Do you not know me, Achi? It is me, it is Andrew."

"I'm sorry," Joseph began to turn away, "I must have made a mistake. I thought you were someone else."

"No, it is me Joseph. Don't you recognize me? I am Shor!" Joseph's eyes began to fill with tears.

Again, Rachel whispered softly in his ear, "The colonel is telling me that his dossier reports that 'Shor' was a nickname when he was young. He must have returned to his given name."

As Rachel continued her communication, Joseph looked at Andrew who appeared to be in a daze—his arms dangled at his sides and his mouth hung open. He had not intended to shoot Joseph. It was only after he had fired the two shots that he realized the pistol was in his hand.

As Joseph continued to move slowly toward Andrew; each step he took caused the settling smoke to swirl at his feet and rise up around his body. Joseph stood directly before him. As Shor's true identity was revealed, he realized that he was talking with a brother of the fraternity, and a friend. What they had prepared for had changed. Taking a slow and deep breath, Joseph began to speak.

The microphone once again broadcast his voice across the hillside, a deafening, thunderous roar that could be heard echoing down the valley. As Joseph softly spoke in his native tongue, he held his arms slightly forward at his side and stretched out his hands so that his palms were fully exposed. It was Joseph's way of letting Andrew know that his intentions were sincere. The words that Joseph began with were familiar, ones that Andrew had heard recited many times.

"No man should enter upon any great or important undertaking without first invoking the blessing of deity." These were words that Joseph lived by and that Andrew had once taught him. But somewhere along the way, Andrew had forgotten the words' meaning. Joseph bowed his head and began a prayer from the book of Psalms.

"Thou O God, knowest our down-sitting and our uprising, and understandest our thoughts afar off. Shield and defend us from the evil intentions of our enemies, and support us under the trials and afflictions we are destined to endure while traveling through this vale of tears."

Sensing some movement around him, but not hearing anything from Rachel, Joseph briefly looked up to see that Hazar and Paul had slowly crept to each side of Andrew. They had both knelt down with their faces disappearing into the smoke covered ground.

Joseph continued, reciting scripture from the book of Job.

"Man that is born of woman is of few days, and full of trouble. He cometh forth as a flower and is cut down; he fleeth as a shadow, and continueth not. Seeing his days are determined, the number of his months are with thee; thou hast appointed his bounds that he cannot pass; turn from that he may rest, until he shall accomplish his day. For there is hope of a tree, if it be cut down, that it will sprout again, and that the tender branch thereof will not cease. But man dieth and wasteth away; yea, man giveth up the ghost, and where is he? As the waters fail from the sea and the flood decayeth and drieth up, so man lieth down, and riseth not up until the heavens shall be no more."

As Joseph was about to conclude, he raised his head and took another look at his surroundings and made sure the three brothers were still kneeling.

Joseph finished the prayer, "Yet O Lord, have compassion on the children of thy creation, administer them comfort in time of trouble, and save them with an everlasting salvation."

As Joseph ended the prayer with the usual "Amen," he thought he heard a faint "so mote it be" from at least one of the three brothers that was kneeling.

Just as Joseph finished with the prayer he heard Rachel's voice in his earpiece. "Infrared has picked up someone moving in the brush on the outskirts of the brow. As soon as I am able to identify who it is, I will let you know." For a moment there was radio silence as Rachel struggled to find and identify the heat signature. After a moment her voice returned, "Joseph it— it's Phillip."

Joseph took another step closer to Andrew and reached out, touching the man's shoulder. "Arise, A'chi."

Andrew looked up at Joseph and stood. The two men were now standing before each other, but Andrew's eyes were downcast, unable to bring himself to face the gaze of the spiritual image of Joseph. Reaching up, Joseph removed the small microphone from his neck, leaned over, and whispered into Andrew's ear.

Still staring at the ground, Andrew could not believe what he had heard. It was a word that he thought he had forgotten; a word that had been buried so deep within his mind that at first he did not understand. But, as Andrew said the word to himself he began to realize its significance and what it had meant to him when he was much younger. *How have I forgotten? What has happened to me through the years that made me turn my back on the ones I loved and that which I held dear?* Andrew could feel the tightness in his chest, and he realized that his eyes were welling with tears. Andrew could not remember the last time that he had wept. *Guilt*—he recognized it for what it was. He had not experienced it in a very long time. Raising his head and now looking at Joseph through his tear-stained eyes, Andrew knew that what he had thought was a spiritual aberration was indeed a real man. More than that, he was a true friend.

Andrew knew that it was Joseph, and he was glad. Thinking that Joseph had been risen from the dead and seeing him stand at the foot of the grave where he and his brothers had buried him, Andrew became overwhelmed with emotions and reached out and pulled Joseph close to his chest and wept on his shoulder. As Andrew stood, Hazar and Paul both leaned back from where they were kneeling and were now sitting on their heels. Neither of them understood what they were seeing, or what was happening. They watched as Andrew and Joseph embraced, as a father would embrace his son. Hazar and Paul both rose to their feet and stood on either side of Joseph and Andrew.

Colonel Asaad looked on through furrowed brows. These actions were disconcerting, but to his credit, he did nothing. Once again Colonel Asaad commanded everyone to continue to maintain radio silence and to stand by.

Joseph's actions were also disturbing to Rachel. This was not a confession; this was barely a military operation. It was a ritual.

Saul. This had the king's signature all over it. There was no doubt now. The king had orchestrated what Rachel recognized as being part ritual and part reparation. Everything that was happening, and everything that had been done—with the exception of Joseph being shot of course—had to be at the direction of King Oman. If Rachel knew Saul like she thought, he would be somewhere close by. He would want to be close so he could see everything as it happened.

Observing Paul and Hazar's apparent confusion, Joseph let go of Andrew's hand and stepped to the other two brothers. Joseph embraced them as he had Andrew. Feeling Joseph's flesh against their own, the two understood, as Andrew had, that Joseph was once again real and alive. To their amazement and pleasure, the younger brothers were sure that the Great Architect of the Universe had raised Joseph from beyond.

Stepping back from Paul and Hazar, Joseph allowed the three brothers to embrace and celebrate what they each thought was sure to be their clemency from the horrid deeds that they had done. Joseph turned and walked back to the foot of the grave and placed his microphone back on his neck. Stretching out his arms, he looked toward the starry night sky and recited a prayer. It was a prayer that Andrew, Paul, and Hazar were familiar with, one that they themselves had prayed many times as they'd grown up in their tiny village. It was the prayer, found in the book of Matthew and again in Luke, that Jesus had recited to his disciples when he gave the Sermon on the Mount. One of his disciples said unto him, Lord, teach us to pray, as John also taught his disciples.

"Our Father, who art in heaven, hallowed be thy Name. Thy kingdom come. Thy will be done, on earth as it is in heaven. Give us this day our daily bread. And forgive us our trespasses, as we forgive those who trespass against us. And lead us not into temptation, but deliver us from evil. For thine is the kingdom, and the power, and the glory, forever and ever. Amen"

22

Having finished the Lord's Prayer, Joseph lowered his arms to his side. Once again, Joseph sensed movement on the outskirts of the brow and could see faint shadows silently moving toward him. Approaching the brow from this side of the hill prohibited almost everyone from realizing that there was any activity taking place. Looking directly past the head of the grave, down beyond where the sprig of acacia had been planted, Joseph recognized a familiar face standing among a group of about eleven or twelve other men.

Well, he had said he would meet them on the hill. Joseph smiled slightly before once again turning off the microphone, and turned back toward the three brothers. "My brothers, I am glad that we have had this chance to reacquaint and share in the joys of life. A lot has happened since the last time that we were all together at the compound, in the rubbish of the temple."

The brothers' eyes cast first to each other and then down to the earth. Their momentary jubilation was sobered. Andrew looked at Paul and Hazar, and turned to Joseph, taking a deep breath, "It is true, Joseph. We have done unspeakable things to you, and to our very souls." His brothers looked on, neither moving to stop the words that poured forth. "For a long time, I have forgotten the meaning of brotherhood, not just within our circle, but within my own blood." Paul and Hazar listened. They couldn't remember a time when Andrew had spoken with such eloquence. "I knew that one day we would be held accountable for our crimes, and we are ready to suffer the consequences of our actions."

Paul was back in the compound, replaying it in his mind. Joseph was coming through the south gate. *Why didn't I just let him leave? We didn't mean to kill you Joseph!* Shaking, the strength in his legs gave out, and he found himself on his knees as tears flowed down his face. "I am scared to even talk to those I called my friends." The group turned toward him, but he couldn't pull his eyes from the ground. "All I can see is my own fear and disgust when I look in their eyes. I cannot live with the burden of what we have done. I tried to be strong like you, brothers, but I'm not. I am weak, and scared, and I cannot carry this! Joseph, were the situation reversed—I would want my attackers brought to justice."

Joseph stood and listened to Paul's confession. "And what would be your punishment for an act as impious as this? What punishment would allow you to look unabashedly into another man's eyes?"

Paul dried his tears as he stood. "The punishment must be equal or greater than that inflicted."

Joseph looked the man in the eye and saw the conviction there. "Even if that punishment was death?" Paul looked at Hazar and then at Andrew.

Wiping the sweat from his brow and standing tall, Paul looked directly at Joseph. "If a peasant such as I have been accessory to the death of so good a man, I think that my throat should be cut from ear to ear, and my tongue should be torn out by the roots and buried in the sands of the sea." Having finished his self-imposed decree, Paul dropped to his knees and lowered his head.

His brothers heard Paul's words, and they stood agape. This was the first time that Andrew could ever remember Paul acting so independently and responsibly.

Turning toward Hazar, Joseph addressed him, "You have heard Paul's confession?"

"Yes, I heard," Hazar replied.

"And are you also willing to stand and abide by the king's ruling pertaining to your participation?"

Hazar moved and placed a hand on Paul's shoulder as he knelt beside him. "Yes, I am willing."

"And what punishment do you think would be fitting for an act as impious as the one that you have committed?"

Hazar thought for a second; the words were not coming easily. "We are a poor family, and through my life I've done what was necessary to survive in a land that never gave unless we made it bleed. We struggle each day for the very bread we eat, and for *enough* to feed our mother and children. Life has been a series of compromising survival and hardship. You ask me for a fitting punishment. I am not sure. But, I know, if someone had taken the life of one of my brothers, I would want to tear their breast open and take their heart for the vultures. I suppose that is all I can expect of you."

Joseph then turned toward Andrew, but before he could pose his question the man spoke. "Joseph, may I speak to my brothers?" Joseph nodded, and Andrew walked to where Hazar and Paul knelt.

"My brothers, I have done many bad things in my life. I think that maybe the worst was that I did not take care of you. When our father died you were too young to understand. Our father gave his life for his country and his people, and the government rewarded him with medals and praise that could not put food on the table. Our mother tried. She worked hard to try and provide for us, but the promises of help for our family were empty. I hated what our father did to us. I resented being treated as an outcast and being poor; hatred filled my heart for his gullibility, and for the lies of our country. I felt that our state had turned its back on us, and I could not forget. Even after the man who we now call father married our mother, I continued to resist. I've resisted all of my life, and now you see where it has gotten me. There are some things you just can't get out of your head. I know what I have done is wrong."

Andrew turned toward Joseph. "It was I that struck the fatal blow. I alone should suffer the consequences." Andrew turned back, leaned down, and kissed each of his brothers on the forehead.

From behind him, Joseph called back his attention. "What do you say then, my old friend? What punishment fits your actions?"

Andrew bowed his head. "I am not an educated man. Hell, I still can't read. Sometimes, it's hard for me to find the right words. But, if I were to impose a sentence for the crime that I alone committed, then I think it should be a most severe punishment. I think the person should have his body cut into pieces and his bowels burned in a fiery furnace so the wind would scatter them throughout the land." Andrew raised his head and turned to Joseph, "That is what I would do, Achi."

Joseph was speechless. The brothers knelt, still and vulnerable before him; they had acknowledged their guilt, and more, their remorse. Just then, the familiar face that Joseph had seen on the opposite side of the brow walked out from the shadows and into the light. He'd slipped into position from the north side of the hill, and his entrance surprised everyone. Everyone except Rachel.

Rachel had not taken her eyes off of Joseph except to check on Phillip, who was still crouched in the brush outskirts of the hill. He was still motionless. *Is he trying to get to Andrew and eliminate him before he could talk? Too late for that.*

Phillip, what are you trying to do? she wondered to herself. She'd run several scenarios through, but none of them seemed to work. She needed the colonel. Rachel radioed Colonel Asaad and asked him to switch over to a prearranged frequency to maintain confidentiality. "Sir, I've sighted an unknown in the brush, believed to be the king's missing man, Phillip. No threatening behavior as of yet, purpose unknown."

The transmission immediately cut out, and Rachel switched back to the sniper's frequency to hear the colonel finishing his command, ". . . perimeter breached, Checkpoint Alpha and Bravo, move in and secure, non-lethal is approved. All others units, stand by for the processions approach."

Checkpoint Alpha was assigned to a two-year veteran of the Special Forces team that went by the code name

Stinger. Checkpoint Bravo was manned by an Israeli soldier, code name Badger. With the chart updated, Rachel's attention was back on Joseph. With the aid of her infrared binoculars she was able to see the familiar face. It was the same familiar face that Joseph had been in communication with just below the horizon of the hill.

Stepping from the shadows into the flickering light, King Saul Oman and his entourage made their presence known. Dressed in full ceremonial regalia, King Oman presented an alarming sight to Andrew and his brothers. The brothers had never seen the king in person, only a few times on television. Regrettably, the brothers now found themselves at center stage, and in the king's presence. As King Oman made his presence known, Joseph turned and bowed.

"How good and pleasant it is for brethren to dwell together in unity." Standing between his brothers Hazar and Paul, Andrew knelt. Each member of the king's entourage was wearing a simple white robe with a piece of twine or cable-tow tied at his waist. Their heads were covered with white draped headscarves with bands, and they each wore plain traditional sandals that were tied with leather straps that ran up to their shins and over their calves.

As the three looked around, they began to recognize faces among the group. Woven into the king's entourage were family, some of whom they had not seen in many years. Slowly their names surfaced in Andrew's mind as he counted them, and he realized they were all there. All twelve of their stepbrothers stood before them, their faces somber and strained. Andrew wondered what his stepfather Israel would think now, seeing all of his boys come together under such a situation. Israel had not been a religious man, but he had a strong conscience. His marriage to their mother, Greta, had been his third and last in his life, but as he looked at his brothers, taking their places in the forming circle around them, he could see Israel imprinted in each of their faces.

The three brothers continued to kneel, and they watched as several of the king's servants set up chairs at various points around the burial site. They had set the king's throne just beyond the foot of the grave at the east end of the brow and set another chair beyond the head of the grave on the west side. The last chair was placed to the south. Each of the twelve brothers that had initially encircled the burial site took up a position along the north side, standing side by side and facing south toward the grave. Once the servants had completed their tasks, they took up positions behind the king, who had taken his place, sitting in the east. The king reached down and picked up a small wooden gavel that was resting on the short podium before him and rapped it once. Sheikh Saleh Ben-Hadad stepped into the flickering light from behind the chair located just beyond the head of the grave at the west end. Bowing, he too took his seat. King Oman then recognized Joseph, asking him to take his place. As Joseph stepped forward, he bowed to the king and then sat down in the chair to the south. All was silent. The only noise that could be heard was the faint and frequent buzzing of the mosquitoes in the night air.

King Oman rose, "The purpose of this gathering is to seek information pertaining to the events that led to the assault and abduction of the overseer of the temple, Brother Joseph Ziegler."

Ben-Zur stepped forward and bowed to the king.

"Some of you have already met brother Ben-Zur. For those of you who have not, he is senior inspector with the Central Police Department. His purpose here tonight is twofold. He will either serve in his official capacity as an inspector with the police, or he will serve as judge advocate for our brotherhood during these proceedings." King Oman then spoke directly to Andrew, Hazar, and Paul. "You may decide to whom you wish to answer; the charges are the same."

Andrew rose to his feet and bowed. "Most Excellent King Oman, I will gladly stand and answer to the charges brought against me by the judge advocate. However, my two younger brothers cannot. They are not under the jurisdiction of the judge advocate and are not bound by the obligations or penalties."

"Are you also willing to stand and answer to the charge of murder?" asked the king.

"I am, Your Majesty."

Upon hearing Andrew's willingness, Joseph rose to his feet. "Might there be two among his brothers who would stand for Paul and Hazar and assume their brothers' place to suffer the consequences of their guilt or reap the rewards of their innocence? That is, if the sheikh concurs with my suggestion?" Joseph asked. As if in deep thought, the sheikh sat for a moment or two without responding.

Finally King Oman spoke, "Sheikh Hadad. Do you concur with the suggestion?"

The sheikh rose to his feet and bowed to the king, "Yes, Your Majesty. I concur with brother Ethan's recommendation." Immediately, there was a strange quiet on the hill.

The inspector quickly recognized the sheikh's error and looked toward Saul.

After a few more moments the sheikh realized that he had misspoken. "I am sorry, Your Majesty. I was just thinking about Joseph's father, Ethan. We prayed together often, and his guidance tonight would have been most welcome. Please forgive an old man for daydreaming. Yes, I agree with Joseph's suggestion."

Ben-Zur reaffirmed in the ritual, "Sheikh Hadad, you concur that if agreed upon by the brothers, the requirements of *the code* will be satisfied?"

The sheikh responded, "Yes, Inspector. This would allow the issues to be resolved by the judge advocate instead of the inspector. By the way, it is good to see you, Inspector. It has been a long time."

Inspector Ben-Zur simply nodded to the sheikh and smiled.

A thin, older yet beardless man stepped forward. "Your Majesty. I am Reuben, Israel's first born. I am authorized to speak on behalf of my brothers. The terms are acceptable."

23

"Joseph, I'm still here." Rachel's soft whisper was soothing as Joseph listened to the charges brought against the brothers. He looked out over the brow toward the tree line to see if he could find her location. "Here, let me give you a little help." Joseph looked down and saw a small red dot slowly making circles on his chest. Rachel was perched high in a tree stand about three hundred meters northwest from the hill. Looking back through the rifle scope he winked at her before turning back to the meeting and stood to give a brief summary of the events that occurred at the compound including his assault and abduction.

"Who will speak and act on behalf of Paul since he is not a member of the Order?" Saul's voice boomed over the clearing.

Reuben replied, "Daniel, son of Israel, and fifth son of Naomi will stand in the place of Paul." Daniel stepped forward and bowed to the king before standing opposite Joseph.

Joseph looked into the man's eyes. "Are the actions that you are about to take of your own free will and accord?"

"They are." Reuben conducted Daniel to a place opposite of where Sheikh Saleh Ben-Hadad sat. The same question was asked and the same answer was returned before the two made their way back to the king to answer again.

Saul pointed toward Paul. "As a result of your brother, Daniel, standing in your place, you are excused and absolved of any crime pertaining to the trial in session." As Paul stood with his other brothers, Daniel knelt next to Hazar and Andrew.

"Who will stand for Hazar?"

"Benjamin, Israel's twelfth son and the youngest child of Miriam will stand for Hazar." The same questions were asked and the like answers given, affirming his readiness.

King Oman spoke to Hazar, "You are also excused and absolved of any crime pertaining to the trial in session." Hazar stepped to the side and stood with his brother as Benjamin knelt down beside Andrew.

"Here, as we meet on a hilltop underneath the starry-decked heavens, one can almost imagine how Jacob, in his vision, saw a ladder extending from earth to heaven." The king's voice was soft, but the night air carried it to the edge of the clearing. "This evening we meet on a level playing field as men have met for hundreds of years when searching for truth and precious common ground. For those of us gathered here, we are once again faced with many dilemmas. We have to decide right from wrong and good from evil. How many times we must venture down this road is not for us to ask. There will always be those who will try to get that which they do not deserve, those who by illegitimate means attempt to get what they cannot legally earn, and those who by betrayal will finally realize that their thirty pieces of silver was simply the price that was paid for a lifetime of shame."

As King Oman finished his remarks he addressed Andrew, "What did you hope to gain by this treachery?" Andrew was slow to speak. Just as the king was about to repeat his question Andrew stood and bowed.

"I have thought a lot about this question, ever since my brothers and I accosted Joseph at the compound. It is as though I have been completely immersed by wanting that which, at the time, I felt was rightfully mine. I am ashamed that I was not and have not been strong enough to prevent the influence by those who I knew had greed in their heart and contempt for the crown."

"Joseph, I've just told Colonel Asaad that Phillip is moving around the east side of the hill toward the king. The colonel has a team member from Alpha moving in now. I'll keep you updated."

Colonel Asaad was almost spitting into the microphone, "Under no circumstances is he to get near the king, Alpha. Lethal force authorized."

The ISS member, code name Stinger, had been waiting for the order. Rachel watched through her thermal as the two heat signatures neared and suddenly became one as they struggled. It was short, and quickly one man was on the ground.

"Check point Alpha come in, Stinger, do you copy?" Crouching, Rachel watched as the standing heat signature returned to a crouched walk, and she continued up the hillside. She was back in the secure channel in a flash.

"Colonel, a heat signature is continuing to move toward the king."

"He took out ISS? Who is he? Bravo, be advised target moving to your position, extremely dangerous, considered armed. This is kill not subdue soldier!"

Rachel recognized the voice as Phillip crackled over the radio. He had Alpha's radio. "Attention, this is the king's personal assistant, stand down. I must reach the king, I . . ."

The radio squawked as the downed ISS gave one last effort, tackling Phillip. In a matter of seconds he was on the ground again. There was no further communication.

"Joseph, if there is some way for you to let the king know that something is wrong, do it. We are trying to handle the situation from here." Joseph stood and was immediately recognized by King Oman.

"Most Excellent King Saul Oman, it would appear that there is a dark cloud approaching from the north. Maybe we should prepare for some bad weather." King Oman looked to the north, and into the clear night sky.

Nodding, the king continued. "Sometimes what the earth needs most is a little rain."

Colonel Asaad stared into his speakers. Did the king want Phillip to reach the summit? Or did the king just have that much confidence in the colonel's team? The colonel rested his chin on his balled fists. His first priority was the king. He had to assume the worst, that Alpha was dead, and that his killer was still making his way toward the brow. "Bravo, you are still green light—eliminate the target."

Bravo was new, but he'd come highly recommended. They'd given him code name Badger. *Please let him be all he was cracked up to be.*

Phillip had moved swiftly toward Bravo position. Sweat beaded on the soldier's forehead as he crouched beneath camouflaged netting. He didn't wipe it away; he barely even breathed as he waited, gripping his combat knife. The faint whispering of brush focused his mind, and he readied his body. He played out his actions in his head, ready to commit. The target was close. Out of the corner of his eye he could see a shadowy figure creeping toward his position. Phillip had followed a small deer path that would lead to the top of the hill. He could hear the man's heavy breathing; he was tired from his engagement with Alpha. The time was now. Darkness aiding his concealment, Bravo lunged from where he had been hiding and grabbed Phillip around the mouth, sinking his knife deep into the man's back.

As Rachel continued to watch she saw a body once again fall, and a heat signature crouched beside it. Her infrared bloomed as a flashlight was turned on and a voice came panting over the airwaves. "My status is green. The target has been neutralized."

"Joseph . . ."

Joseph stood again and repeated Rachel's words in his ear, "Your Majesty, it looks as if the cloud has dissipated."

The king looked at Joseph and then looked to the north horizon. Joseph smiled, bowed to the king, and sat back down.

24

With Badger's successful elimination of the threat, Colonel Asaad advised all Special Forces units to step down to standby status. "Rachel, remain at your position. I'm posting Dotson as a spotter. Channel four is now reserved; the rest of Bravo Squad, move up to retrieve Phillip. Alpha, move in and get Stinger."

Rachel flipped over to channel four and made contact with her counterpart; he was positioned on the other side of the hill. Together they had full sweep of the area, but only about half each.

The king had walked to Andrew and asked him to approach so that he might answer his charges. Andrew stood, walked to a position before the king and knelt. The sheikh spoke across the hill, reading the charges, as the king looked on.

Rachel's eyes focused on the two squads as they made their way toward Alpha and Bravo checkpoints, and he noticed that Badger was on the move. Badger had reported green status. *Did Phillip take him out after the communication?* Her visual was moving out of sight now. She radioed over, asking if the other spotter had him marked, and he responded with a negative. *Dammit.* Sliding from her position, she slung her rifle over her shoulder and broke into a run, trying to gain a better flank. "Sir, a heat signature is on the move from Bravo position, requesting permission to move to a better position." She left out the fact that she was already breathing hard from her run.

Suddenly, Badger's voice was back on the radio, "Negative, Bravo checkpoint is still green. Repeat—Bravo checkpoint is green." There was something off in his voice. He was more than winded; he was holding back real pain.

"Rachel, this is Colonel Asaad. Maintain position. Bravo is green, re-confirm movement." Rachel was nowhere near her last position now, and the heat signature was still around the north side of the hill—she couldn't reconfirm. But she certainly couldn't hold her position. She kept running.

Having finished reading the charges, Sheikh Ben-Hadad bowed to the king and sat down. King Oman stood and began pacing the area near the grave. As he circled the kneeling brothers, he began a story. It was a story of love—a love so great that no mere mortal could fully comprehend it. As he continued to talk, he stopped directly in front of Andrew and asked him to stand. Andrew looked up at the king and did as he was commanded; the king held out his hands. Andrew reached up and took hold of Saul and stood.

"Andrew, I understand the great pressures that you and your brothers Hazar and Paul have been made to bear. I'm sorry for the struggles your families have had to endure and the compromises that you've had to make. I know the sacrifice that this country asked of your father, and continues to ask of its people." The king took his left hand and extended it toward Joseph, who stood and approached them. They met near the center of the brow, and as Joseph took his place, he could see the tears that fell from Andrew's eyes. As if it were the most natural thing to do, Andrew reached out and embraced Joseph upon the five points of fellowship. He embraced him as a son would embrace his father or a mother her child.

As Andrew took a step back, Joseph clasped hands with him. "I know that temptation can be a terrible thing, and worse if we blind ourselves into seeing it as opportunity. I know that this man, this Judas, is one who can offer much, but know there is also forgiveness in the world, and those who will help their friends. We know that it is this Judas who has betrayed our king, and we know who he is. This man who has been seeking his thirty pieces of silver is in our midst."

As Joseph spoke, he was staring directly at the sheikh, who looked from Joseph, to Andrew, to Saul. Suddenly, the cool night air had become humid and sticky, and Hadad felt small beads of sweat collect on his forehead. The sheikh's heart was beating fast as he slowly rose from his seat. Gripping the arms of the chair, he pulled himself to his feet, his hand reaching into the recesses of his robes.

At that moment, Badger burst out into the open from the brush, a shadowy figure on the hillside. Blood ran down his side as he moved slowly toward the flickering lanterns, cradling his side. His vision was blurry as he struggled up the hill. Just before he'd managed to plunge his knife in

Phillip's back, the man had managed a deft twist and sunk his own knife into Badger's ribs. The sheikh caught sight of the soldier running toward them.

Badger kept low and to the east, trying to keep in the sniper's blind spot as he staggered toward the brow. "EVERYONE! REMAIN CALM! NOBODY MOVE!" Badger shook his head to clear his vision, and King Oman came into focus.

Badger pulled his pistol, and in one smooth movement aimed and fired. As the gun leveled, Andrew shoved the king to the ground, putting himself in the bullet's path. With a grunt, Andrew went down. He'd given Joseph the time he needed, and as Badger lined up another shot, Joseph lunged forward into the man's injured side. The jolt of pain knocked the weapon from his hand, which went twisting out and into the darkness. Badger fell on top of Joseph, knocking the wind out of him. Badger moved quickly, planting a knee in Joseph's chest, and sprang back to his feet.

Circling around to the right, Badger spotted the king lying beneath Andrew, struggling to shift the man's weight. He snatched up one of the oil lanterns within the circle and flung it toward the brothers who were rushing to the king's aid. Burning oil spewed out, and soon the grass and brush around them were aflame. The diversion allowed Badger a few extra seconds to close. Reaching down to his boot, Badger drew the blood-stained knife that he had used on Phillip. Ben-Zur and Andrew's brothers circled around the flames, but they weren't fast enough. Badger pulled the king from under Andrew's body and held the knife to his throat. "Back off, all of you!"

"Do as he says." The king's voice was calm and authoritative. With the blade to Saul's throat, the onlookers backed down the hill. Badger commanded them to stop just far enough away to where he could still see them.

With his hands before him, Joseph moved forward. "This started as a ceremony of peace; it can still end that way." Badger just laughed, as he watched Sheikh Ben-Hadad advancing slowly from behind. Taking advantage of the diversion, the sheikh managed to move in behind Joseph and pulled a long, slim dagger from beneath his robes, raising it high over his head.

As Saul struggled against his captor, Badger's knife traced a thin line of blood against his throat. "Joseph! Behind you!"

Joseph turned and faced the sheikh, dagger raised and ready to strike. "All we needed from you was the scrolls, but just like your father, you act the fool. Here is the result of your pride!"

As the knife plunged toward Joseph's upraised hands, a sudden vacant look filled the sheikh's eyes, and his head cocked sideways. The knife fell from his hands as his body crumpled at Joseph's feet. He was dead before he hit the ground.

Heartbreak was visible on Badger's face as the body fell. "Father!"

Joseph dived for the dagger and rose to a crouch, but Badger's tear-streaked face was a mask of rage as he screamed. "Stop right there Joseph! I will cut his throat from one ear to the other before you're able to reach me!" Joseph dropped the blade, brushed the dirt from his hands, and stood facing the sheikh's son. Badger had shifted Saul to be a better shield, the knife still pressed tightly against his throat. "They wouldn't dare shoot at me while I have you, Your Majesty!"

"Look around!" Anger played in Joseph's voice as he pleaded, "Don't you realize there is no way out?"

"You're right, Joseph, there is no way out. Watch your king bleed like the pig he is!"

Saul's voice suddenly cut in, "If killing the king is your goal, then you have made a serious error." Joseph caught his eye.

"What are you talking about?" Badger snarled.

"I am not the king." Saul looked to Joseph.

Joseph stepped slowly forward. "He is telling the truth. We did it to protect the real king from his assassins. You can kill that man, but his name is not Saul Oman; he is Tom Finn, a royal body double."

For a moment Badger was silent, before a laughter rolled out of him. He was feeling dizzy now, and stars obscured in his vision. His entire side, which had been warm from blood, was now cold and prickling. His voice was slurred as he said, "If he's not the king, then where is he?"

"Your father knew who the real king was," Saul continued.

"My father is dead!" shouted Badger.

"I know. He died while trying to kill the king."

Slowly, Badger's vision focused on Joseph and the sheikh's body at his feet.

Hesitant at first, Saul slowly raised his right hand and pointed his finger toward Joseph. "There, there he is. There is the rightful heir to the throne. There is the king. Didn't you see? Sheikh Hadad was trying to kill Joseph!"

Badger shoved Saul away and lunged at Joseph, knocking him to the ground and grabbing his throat, the point of the knife resting between his ribs.

"What I do, I do in the name of my father!" But, as he looked down, his prisoner was laughing.

Badger blinked hard to clear his vision. "What? You're going to die, you know that? You're going to die, Oman!"

Looking up at Badger, Joseph softly said, "There are two things you should know. One, I am not the king, he—," Joseph pointed to where Saul had risen, "always was and always will be my king, and three hundred and sixty-five days from this exact moment, you, my young friend, will have been dead exactly one year."

As Badger reared back to plunge the blade into Joseph's chest, a small 7.62 millimeter projectile had already been sent on its journey. Faster than sound, it cut through the night air, entered through Badger's forehead, and continued its voyage through his skull. The small serrated shrapnel tore apart the fleshy tissue of the brain and finally came to a sudden stop, embedded in the back wall of the soldier's skull.

The velocity of the projectile knocked his body backward; his spasming fingers released the knife that, only seconds before, had been about to end Joseph's life. From her position, ninety degrees from her original location, Rachel let her breath out in a sigh and rested her head against the scope of her rifle. She'd disobeyed a direct order to remain put, and that wasn't something that was done in the Sayeret Matkal, but Joseph and Saul were safe.

Colonel Asaad and the rest of his team swarmed the hilltop, closely followed by Inspector Ben-Zur.

"Saul, are you all right?" The king took a moment to collect his thoughts before he reached up and grasped Joseph's proffered hand.

Seeing Colonel Asaad approaching, Joseph bowed to the king and excused himself.

"Colonel, don't you think that's cutting it just a little close?"

"I'm sorry, Your Majesty, I had no idea that a mole could have gotten this deep into our organization."

The king placed a hand on his shoulder. "Their loyalty had been predetermined long ago by something much more powerful than king and country."

"Your Majesty?"

"Blood, Colonel. Unlike Judas, the promises made were for much more than just thirty pieces of silver."

25

The inspector approached at a jog, coming to a stop and giving a small bow. "Ah, Inspector, I was just about to go looking for you."

"I am here, Your Majesty," the inspector huffed.

The king shook his hand, "Well, it looks as though you can finally close the case on Ethan's murder."

Ben-Zur smiled at him. "Yes, Your Majesty. I'm sorry that I could not have done more."

"Just having the law as witness will do more in the world of politics than you know, my friend."

Joseph found Hazar and Paul at their fallen brother's side. Joseph checked for a pulse and found that he was still alive. The injury was superficial, and already the blood flow from his arm had stemmed. Joseph gave a shout for a medic.

Regaining consciousness, Andrew looked up at Joseph. "I am sorry my old friend. Can you forgive me?"

Joseph smiled. "Don't worry, everything worked out just as it was supposed to. There is nothing to forgive."

A few meters from where Andrew lay, the king and the inspector knelt down near the sheikh's body. "We'll need to find transport for the body; he needs to be cared for appropriately. Despite what has happened here, he was a popular man, and things can still go sour if we don't tread carefully. He gave this country more than fifty years of his life; we should honor him in his death."

It had taken Rachel several minutes to get back to the hill and find Joseph. She found him explaining to the three brothers the entirety of the ruse. His shirt was open, and Hazar was tracing the two slugs that were lodged in the Kevlar. "But you never even flinched!"

Joseph looked at Andrew. "I'm just glad that you only fired twice."

Andrew motioned for Joseph to come closer. As Joseph leaned down, Andrew pulled him close. "My brother, I only had two rounds or I'd have kept pulling the trigger. You scared the life out of me!" The brothers laughed as Rachel caught Joseph in an embrace.

Suddenly, from the north side of the hill a shadowy figure emerged from the wood line and stumbled into the open. It was a man. He was shouting at the top of his lungs, "WHERE IS MY KING?"

Instantly the Special Forces un-slung their weapons and were moving in the direction of the threat. King Oman heard the commotion and took off in the direction of the shouting.

"Don't shoot! Please, don't shoot!" As the king reached Phillip, the soldiers lowered their weapons.

Phillip collapsed in the king's arms. "I am sorry, Your Majesty. It took me longer to get here than I had anticipated."

"Do not worry, Achi. You have done well."

"The sheikh's son—he's a member the ISF. He was put on this assignment. I came as fast as I could."

"It is all right, Achi, we know about Badger; do not worry my friend."

"No, Your Majesty, there is more, a daughter—Hadashah."

"Hadashah was the sheikh's daughter?"

Colonel Asaad stepped toward the king. "We have yet to find her body. We're still searching the area. The villagers told us there are a lot of cave systems in that area."

The king was having a hard time holding on. Phillip's back was slick and warm. The king's eyes widened. "Help! We need a medic!" Immediately ISF members took him from the king and began to dress the wound. Colonel Asaad had radioed for a medevac helicopter from Tel Nof Airbase, only fifteen minutes away.

As the helicopter landed, they helped Phillip, Andrew, and the hurt member from Alpha team into the belly of the transport. Two more helicopters from Colonel Asaad's 118th Squadron silently hovered overhead. As they touched down, the king boarded one, which lifted off immediately. Hazar and Paul gave one last thanks for his forgiveness, and Joseph watched as all fourteen of Andrew's brothers banded together and walked down the hill. Seeing them leave together, Joseph knew how lucky they were to have each other.

Turning, he and Rachel embraced, kissing until Colonel Asaad was forced to interrupt.

"Captain Barack, attention!" Rachel turned to face her commander, clicking her heals. "Do you remember when I ordered you to maintain your position?"

"Yes sir." Rachel set her jaw.

"And do you remember when I then ordered you to continue on foot, at your recommendation, to get a better line of sight on an unconfirmed enemy?"

Rachel paused, "No sir."

"Well you had better start remembering that part, because that's what it is going to state in the report. It is also going to state that had this plucky young captain *not* made such a suggestion, and had she *not* followed her superior's order to act on that suggestion, she would have violated the right to call herself a soldier, and we would have lost the king of this country."

Colonel Asaad turned to Rachel, held out his hand, and smiled as Rachel shook. "Captain Barack, not only are you one of the finest Special Forces members I have ever had the privilege of knowing, but that was the best damn shooting I have ever seen."

"Thank you, Colonel."

"Now I suggest you two get some rest. Dismissed, and as for you Joseph, I'll see you at lodge."

Joseph returned his salute and simply said, "Shalom."

As the colonel boarded his waiting humvee, a voice buzzed in Rachel's ear. "Rachel, are you there?" It was Saul.

"Saul, it's so good of you to call. I thought I had missed saying good-bye to you."

"This isn't goodbye Rachel. I just wanted to let you know that Joseph and I couldn't have pulled this off without you. All that experience saving us as children really paid off. Don't you agree?"

"It was nothing, Your Majesty. You know that's what I do."

"I know, and you do it so very well. Listen Rachel, there should be one last bird to pick you up." Rachel looked at the waiting helicopter with a raised eyebrow.

"And, where are you sending us worn-out heroes now, Your Majesty?"

"Well, there is one stop for you to make, but then you and Joseph have a good time back in Haifa. Your room is still waiting for you."

Rachel's eyes lit up as she jumped back into Joseph's arms; he just stared dumbfounded but smiled back at her. "Thank you Saul. Joseph and I still have a lot of catching up to do."

"I'll talk with you later. Oh, and give my regards to the flight crew. I think you all know each other."

As the radio died away, she looked at Joseph. "That was Saul. He said the bird was for us and that our room in Haifa was paid for."

As the door opened they heard a familiar "Oh baby!" Even the dusk light somehow managed to shine off Todd's forehead as he welcomed them aboard. As Joseph and Rachel climbed into their seats and strapped in, the pilot looked back from the cockpit, raising his visor.

"So I hear we're going to a hotel in Haifa. Think they'll have some sweet iced tea? Joseph, what in the world are you wearing?"

"Well," Joseph looked at his Kevlar and robe, "it's a ceremonial robe. And pertaining to your next question, don't ask. It's a long story."

Keith just nodded. "Are we all in?"

As Todd pulled the side door closed, Keith powered up the helicopter. They quickly rose up and over the hills, heading west out across the desert toward the Port of Haifa.

26

Under the guidance of Captain Kelly, the helicopter moved swiftly away from the brow of the hill. Joseph and Rachel settled back for what they hoped would be a smooth and short ride. Todd's voice came in through their headsets over the roar of the rotors, "We're about to make a pit stop. Then we'll be back on schedule to Haifa." He smiled before turning to face the front again as the helicopter began a steep descent. A warning buzzer went on for a moment before Keith corrected, "Huh, sorry about that—bird's a little heavier than I thought." As they lightly touched down, and the whine of the blades died away, Joseph could hear Keith speaking on a different frequency.

". . . this is Pegasus. Do you copy?" Keith's head bobbed as he listened. "Omega-Seven be advised—Pegasus has landed. Adam and Eve are in the garden."

Joseph laughed, "Did you say our call sign is Pegasus?" Todd nodded with a raised eyebrow. Joseph just laughed and leaned back in his chair.

Todd had already hopped out, and as he swung his door shut, Joseph and Rachel looked out the side windows, but they could only see dust swirling around them. Except for the landing lights on the helicopter, all was dark.

Todd again came over the speakers, "All clear here. I'll open the door when the rotors stop turning." After another two or three minutes, the side door slid open, and Keith cut the main power. With the helicopter silent, Todd helped Rachel and Joseph out and proceeded to secure and anchor the bird. Keith climbed out of the cockpit and gave them each a proper greeting.

"Keith, what are we doing here?" Rachel looked around.

Keith looked down at his watch and pulled a small flashlight from his jacket pocket. "Hang on just a minute. Yeah, we need to get moving. We'll be there in a few minutes." Shining his flashlight ahead of them, Keith led Joseph and Rachel into a remote, heavily wooded area, where the slope descended a few hundred meters down a small ravine.

Joseph stopped. "Keith, where are you taking us?"

"Just bear with me. I promise you, we'll be there soon."

"Keith!"

"Look, just relax, you two. What, you don't trust me? I'd tell you if I could, but it's above my pay grade."

Shaking his head, Joseph continued to follow their guide into the darkness. Todd had caught up, carrying his own flashlight, and was bringing up the rear. After a few more minutes, Keith retrieved a small two-way radio from his jacket pocket.

"Omega-Seven this is Pegasus. Adam and Eve are at the gate," he said into the radio.

"Pegasus, ten-four, please stand by," came the reply.

Rachel chimed in, "Keith, are you going to tell us what's going on?"

Before Keith could respond, loud booms echoed from behind the nearby rock formation, triggering a memory that Joseph had buried many years ago. Light began to emerge from behind the rocks, revealing an opening in the mountain. Joseph realized they were standing in a doorway. He reached and took hold of Rachel's hand. "I've been here before." From inside the doorway a voice shouted to them.

"Indeed, Joseph. You have been here many times. And now it is time for you to come home!"

Joseph did not hesitate. He ran straight through the doorway and down a flight of steps, pulling Rachel along with him. At the bottom of the steps, the lighted entrance gave way to darkness, and for a moment Rachel thought she saw a darker shadow moving within it.

"Hello, is someone there?" she asked.

Suddenly, small overhead lights began to flicker on, one after another. At first, they seemed like twinkling stars, bright and far away, but slowly the room was revealed to be a great hall, and the earth-formed vaulted ceiling loomed high overhead.

Rachel squeezed Joseph's hand. "I remember this place. The lights weren't here before. Look Joseph—there they are."

Joseph let his eyes drift in the direction she was pointing. "Am I dreaming?"

"I can see them too, Joseph. You're not dreaming. They are real."

Joseph softly whispered the names out loud as he looked at each one, "Jachin—Boaz." Before him sat the two pillars that had originally sat on the porch of King Solomon's temple—the two pillars that King Solomon himself had commissioned. Joseph knew them well. The one on the left was Boaz and the one on the right was Jachin. Each pillar was almost six feet thick and stood more than twenty-five feet tall, and chapiters adorned their tops. Fashioned out of molten brass by the cunning Hiram, the son of a widow from the tribe of Naphtali, King Solomon had personally commissioned him to do the work. According to scripture, Hiram was credited with naming them.

Joseph ran over and began circling them, examining every angle. His eyes darted back and forth from one to the other. Again, he looked toward the tops of the pillars near the ceiling to see the two rows of lilies, the network, and the two hundred pomegranates that the widow's son had fashioned around each chapiter. Memories began to unravel in the back of his mind; the images in his head entwined with reality and suddenly he was twelve again.

He, Saul, and Rachel were standing at the bottom of the pillars. They were counting the pomegranates. They had counted them many times to see if there were really two hundred around each one, and somehow they always managed to lose track. They could never remember where they had started counting.

"Are they as you remember them to be, Achi?" Saul asked, stepping into the hall from the lit stairwell behind them, a smile across his face. At first, Joseph could not speak. For as long as he could remember, he'd thought the Great Hall and the two pillars were a dream. Their half memory had haunted him for most of his adult life. Now, once again in the presence of the two massive structures, events from his childhood had slowly started to bloom into memories. Memories buried so deep that Joseph was unaware they'd ever been forgotten snapped into place, creating a timeline—a history—of who he was. There were so many, like a dam bursting. It was hard to piece them together in the right order. Once again he had visions of three small children running around a great hall laughing and giggling. He could remember running his hands across the cavern walls, their games, seeing for the first time the great pillars and feeling how cold the brass was to the touch. Slowly, Joseph sank to his knees, tears rolling down his face, as Rachel moved to his side.

"Joseph, I didn't want you to think that this was not real. We had a lot of fun playing around in here when we were children. Do you remember?"

"Do *you* remember Rachel? How we used to chase you and pull your hair?"

"Of course I remember—and yank my hair was more like it." Rachel lifted Joseph's chin and softly caressed his brow with her hand.

"Rachel, I remember. I remember what I asked you about in Haifa." He raised his head to look her in the eyes. "We were two small children standing in the shadow of two massive pillars pledging that our hearts would always belong to each other."

Rachel wiped away his tears, and her own. "Mon *amour*, everything is going to be all right," she said as he wrapped her arms around his neck. "I am right here with you Joseph. I will always be with you."

Saul knelt down opposite them. "Well seeing as we are all sitting, perhaps I can tell you all a story about how all this got started, and about how it needs to end."

27

"I remember when we discovered this passage in the mountains when we were children. We had no idea that it would lead us to this hall and to one of the greatest archeological discoveries ever found. Do you remember what you called this room Rachel?"

Rachel nodded, "The chamber of truth."

"I couldn't get over how perfect that name was. After the parchments were deciphered, it seems almost like fate. The parchments had been treated with a salve to prevent decay, and they told what had really happened to the king's temple and how the pillars ended up in the Great Hall. Rachel, you read us a good portion of them as kids—how the prophet Jeremiah had predicted the destruction of Jerusalem, and that the Babylonians would eventually destroy the great temple. This prediction lead to the development of a plan for the removal of the most treasured artifacts, including Jachin and Boaz. The two massive pillars had been painstakingly disassembled, transported and reassembled in the great hall. And although these two pillars are possibly the greatest archaeological find in world history, they are not the most important." Saul rose and began circling the pillars. "Isn't that right, Rachel?"

Rachel kept her eyes on the marbled floor, knowing Saul wasn't looking for an answer.

"The most significant find was that of a special parchment that Rachel had easily been able to decipher. It was a written parchment, which indicated the true lineage from the time of King Solomon's reign to a point of only eighty years before the time three small adventurous children made the discovery of a lifetime."

Saul was frowning and had his hands folded behind his back. "Everything would have been fine, had it not been for an exchange student who contacted me seeking information for a paper he was writing. The paper had something to do with my great grandfather, King William, and he wanted some simple clarification on the spelling of a name. Apparently the student had discovered through some research that there existed two different spellings for the name of the young man who was heir to the throne. The young man whose name was in question was William's oldest son Aaron. The student wanted to know if Aaron was spelled with one "A" or with two.

Being interested in my family history, I, of course, said I would personally look into it. Subsequently, I discovered what, at first, appeared to be a discrepancy in the archives at the hall of records. However, after doing a little more research, I found something astonishing. Several documents from King William's personal scribe talked about the king having two sons. Further evidence supported these facts, and when I found a diary from my great grandmother there was a handwritten notation."

The king paused and looked toward the ceiling. "It read to the effect that the king's wife gave birth to two healthy boys with the help of Sala, a midwife. The boys were identical twins. She assumed that the king would be overjoyed upon arriving home, and she received word from him to name the firstborn Aaron with two As and his second son Aron with only one A. To make matters worse it was found that Sala, the midwife who had assisted the queen, had not made the proper arrangements to keep the two separate. At that time, it was customary in the royal family upon the birth of twins, for the first born to be placed in a purple shawl and the next twin to be placed in either a blue or crimson. When King William had returned and had entered into the royal nursery, there were both of his sons, Aaron and Aron; both sons were wrapped in purple. No name tags, no arm bands, no special features, and no way to determine who was first born. King William was enraged. How could he know which son was the legal heir to the throne? Neither their mother nor the midwife could tell which was which. A decision had to be made, and King William wasted no time in making it.

"One of the boys would be raised as Prince Aaron and was provided all the luxuries of the throne as the son of a king. The other twin would be raised as the son of the midwife who had made the terrible blunder. There could be no question which was the rightful heir. The king's son would be Aaron, and the midwife's would be spelled Aron. He would be raised as the son of a simple commoner. As I traced Sala's son's path through accounts, diaries, and birth records, I found that Aron had raised his own family in a small village just outside the palace, and that Aron's wife had given birth to only one child, a son named Ethan."

Rachel glanced at Joseph. "Saul, are you saying that all of this cloak and dagger business has been about the *scrolls?*" asked Rachel.

"How much do you remember, Achi?" Saul asked, his eyes piercing Joseph.

Joseph turned toward Saul, and after a brief pause he said, "Everything. I remember everything."

Saul stood up and walked over to the far side of the pillar to Boaz. "I'm amazed at how one little inquiry can create so much confusion in the temple; clearly my biggest mistake was to seek counsel from Sheikh Hadad. At first I wasn't sure—I thought perhaps the sheikh was attempting to turn me against my friends, but then he attacked you. He truly believed his words; perhaps he knew more than I did. Now Joseph, it is time to end this. I need you to give the scrolls up."

Joseph looked up at the king and asked, "What are you talking about?"

"Don't be so insolent! You know exactly what I'm talking about!" exclaimed Saul. "Where are they?"

Joseph looked at Rachel. "Please tell our friend that I don't have the foggiest idea what he is talking about."

"I cannot believe—after all these years—that the one person I would lay down my life for would do this. You have betrayed me Joseph. *You* are my Judas!" As the king shouted, he had grabbed Joseph by the breast of his shirt with both of his hands, shouting into Joseph's face. Joseph did not retaliate; instead, he collapsed to his knees.

From the ground Joseph spoke, "Now I see. At the compound, they weren't asking for my soul. They wanted the scroll. Speaking in English, I couldn't tell. And for who, Saul? Who sent those men to find me? Who cast doubt that I would have something to do with them?" Joseph could feel his temper starting to rise. Gritting his teeth and clenching his fists, he stood up and leaned in, within inches from Saul's face.

"Do you really believe that I want to be something other than your friend and brother? How dare you, Saul? You question my allegiance with your talk of deceit. You attack my honor with your words of betrayal." Joseph began to circle Saul as he continued. "You misrepresent my integrity by categorizing me as a Judas? What is it that you think I want? I was beaten, knocked unconscious, and left for dead. Oh no. Make no mistake, Your Majesty; it is not I that is the Judas here!"

Remembering how Joseph and Saul used to fight as boys, Rachel stepped between them. Taking Joseph by the arm, she led him away from Saul and toward the center of the great hall.

"Joseph, what are you saying? You think I had something to do with what happened to you at the compound? Achi, don't you understand? When I heard what had happened it was almost more than I could bear. I was filled with so much hate and disgust that I wanted to annihilate everyone involved. Having lost you in the Palestinian conflict, I couldn't think of losing you again. This is my fault! After I had shared that information with Sheikh Hadad, he suggested that we compare it to the information that was contained within the scrolls. When we opened the special vault that your father had built to house the scrolls, we discovered the ones containing the true lineage were missing."

"And you thought that since my father had built the special vault . . ."

"It was the sheikh that guessed that your father had shared the secret access code of the vault with you. His was—very convincing. I believed him when he assured me that there could be no one else who could have removed them."

Rachel had been listening quietly. "Saul, when did you discover this so-called lineage scroll missing?" Saul turned to face her.

"Sheikh Hadad and I discovered it missing after we were in the Hall of Records." Rachel burst out laughing.

"What is so amusing?" Saul asked.

"Let me ask you, Saul. Who cataloged the scrolls after we found them? How did the sheikh even know about them? We only told your father."

"Rachel, you know that was more than twenty-five years ago. How am I supposed to know what my father did? He told me never to mention the scrolls again, and I never did. He was an honorable man. I had no reason to access my father's vault." Having finished his explanation, Saul kneeled down on the steps leading up to the two pillars and sat down.

Once again Joseph spoke, "Let me remind the king that my father was also an honorable man. And just like me, he would never have betrayed his king's trust. Not to me, or anyone else. My father never spoke to me about anything that took place in the palace or anything that involved the Royal family."

Joseph walked over to where the king was sitting. "Your Majesty?" The king did not move. "Saul, I know that there is something you want to ask me. Go ahead. Ask."

There was a moment of silence. "Achi, if you did not take the scrolls, then who could have removed them?" Joseph turned his head and looked over at Rachel before turning his attention back to Saul. "We assume that the scroll never made it into the vault to begin with. I can think of but one person who could have taken the scrolls. But like my father I would never betray the trust of someone I loved."

Saul looked up at Joseph. "I guess it would be foolish of me to demand that you tell me. I'm sure that if the situation were reversed, I would probably do the same thing."

Joseph stepped past Saul and back up onto the porch and walked between the two great pillars. He gazed up at them as he had done many times before. "Saul, look at these two magnificent structures. Jachin and Boaz. Still as magnificent as when we first found them. Do you remember what Rachel used to call them?"

Saul rose to his feet. "Oh yes. I seem to recall that she had several different names for them. Sometimes they were Tom and Huck, or Athos and Porthos, and sometimes Robin Hood and Little John. Something about how we thought we were invincible, immortal, and bigger than life."

"We were both much younger then. Now we know that we are not invincible, and I am certain that I am not immortal. How old were we, Saul, eleven? Maybe twelve? I can't remember. But I do remember the scrolls.

Saul, your great grandfather and mine were one in the same, William. And both of our grandfathers were named

Aaron. Yours with two As and mine with one. Regardless of which of them was born first, our great grandfather, our king, had a difficult decision to make. Without certain proof of which was first, there would be constant turmoil within the kingdom. History has shown throughout the ages, brother has fought against brother for power. It happened with Cain and Abel, Ishmael and Isaac, Jacob and Esau, and countless others. Saul, our great grandfather did not want there to be reason for contention between his sons. If he were here today, I'm sure that he wouldn't want there to be any contentious feelings between you and me. He did the only thing that he knew to do. Maybe he got it right, and maybe he didn't. It doesn't matter. It doesn't take away from the fact that my father loved me as his father loved him, just as King Caro loved you. And like you, I wouldn't trade that for anything."

Joseph turned and laid his hands on Saul's shoulders. "Saul, my old and dearest friend, you are the rightful heir to the throne. You are my king." As Joseph had finished speaking he stood and bowed.

Saul sighed and extended his hand. "Will you help an old friend up?"

"Of course I will, Your Majesty."

"Thank you, Achi. You know Joseph, sometimes I think that the crown *would* fit your head better than it does mine."

"I am always at your disposal, Your Majesty."

As he stood, Saul caught sight of the pendant that had slipped from beneath Joseph's robe. "With your memories coming back, have you remembered where that jewel came from yet?"

Joseph took hold of the jewel and held it away from his neck, looking it over. "I just thought you had one of the craftsmen make it. I never really thought about it much."

"Joseph, look at it. Look at it closely. I bet Rachel knows where it came from. I seem to remember seeing a jewel that looked very much like that one around the neck of an old skeletal friend of ours many years ago. I believe he was guarding a chest of ancient scrolls."

"No! This is that jewel?" asked Joseph.

"Not only is that the jewel Joseph, but also that is one of the last few remaining artifacts still in existence from King Solomon's temple. It is believed to have been worn by *Hiram* himself."

Once again Joseph extended his hand, and Saul extended his. They embraced and whispered into each other's ear and stepped back bowing. Smiling, they began to laugh aloud.

Saul shook his head. "Oh that reminds me. I almost forgot. Joseph, your friend David, the jeweler, tried to contact you. Apparently your watch has turned up. It was pawned to him by three brothers just before they made their way to the hill."

Smiling, Joseph bowed again and, taking Rachel by the hand, started walking with her toward the stairwell.

Rachel pulled Joseph close. "What was all that whispering about?"

"Oh nothing," Joseph said. "I just let the king know that you were still my girl."

Rachel laughed. "Well, what did Saul say?"

"He told me that it wasn't too late to trade. That I could still have the kingdom if I wanted it." Rachel wrapped her arms around Joseph's neck and gave him a warm kiss on his lips. As Joseph pushed the stairwell door open, Rachel suddenly stopped and looked above her head.

"Joseph, look! Can you believe that thing is still there?" Protruding from the doorway, a cracked and weathered arrow stuck out from the woodwork.

"Oh yeah, I knew it was there. Saul and I had a discussion about that arrow."

As Saul stepped into the stairwell behind them he said, "If you will, just think back for a minute, Rachel. You'll realize that was the *last* arrow that I ever shot in your direction. Joseph can be quite convincing when he wants to drive a point home." Rachel turned and looked toward Joseph and then back to Saul. Joseph was shaking a balled fist.

"Joseph, you broke Saul's nose didn't you? I remember that! Saul, you said that you fell and hit a table."

"Yes, well, punched, fell—the difference is only in the semantics." Saul, who had walked back to the great hall, was now standing between the two pillars.

"Look Rachel," Joseph whispered as he motioned for her to turn around. "There they are, the three great pillars, together again: Jachin, Boaz, and King Saul Oman."

After a brief pause Joseph turned back to Rachel, "And here I am with the crown jewels. I've got to be the luckiest man alive."

"Joseph, you're going to make me cry. Thank you for loving me."

"I do love you Rachel, I've always loved you. And I always will."

As Joseph and Rachel walked into the open air, he whispered into Rachel's ear, "You still have that scroll don't you?"

Rachel just cocked her head back. "Joseph, you know that a girl never kisses and tells."

The night was still and dark; the illumination from the stairwell cast the only light in a pool around them. Rachel stopped laughing and put a hand on Joseph's arm, suddenly as silent as the night around them. Tentatively, she called out, "Todd? Keith?"

A spray of automatic weapon fire cut loose just above their heads as they dove to the ground, branches and shrubs snapping around them like toothpicks. With them no longer holding the door, it swung shut, and utter blackness descended. Joseph's dive took him into the bushes, where he landed atop something that groaned.

Todd's expletives were muffled by his gag, but Joseph's mind was focused on one thing. *Rachel, where's Rachel?* The night was silent again—had she taken off? That would be her instinct—going alone, a guerilla fighter. Todd's eyes flickered open, and relief flooded his face at seeing Joseph. Joseph snatched the man's two-way from his belt and whispered over the radio. "Pegasus to Omega-Seven!"

"Pegasus, go ahead. This is Omega-Seven."

"Omega-Seven, be advised, we are outside and we are taking enemy fire."

Immediately, Saul responded, "Ten-four. Message received and understood. Is everyone OK?"

"I'm unable to advise. Have two accounted for but the fair maiden's whereabouts are unknown."

"Ten-four, sit tight."

As Saul finished his transmission Joseph caught the glimpse of someone moving just below their position. He pulled the gag from his friend's mouth. "Do you have a weapon? Who the hell is out there?" The response Joseph received was not the one that he wanted to hear.

"It's Hadashah," Todd hissed. "She must have been at the hill and stowed on board when we took off. That's why the helicopter was heavier than we thought. And no, *she* has my gun." Todd and Joseph just looked at each other.

Looking back down the hill, Joseph could make out a silhouette closing in. Now, only about ten to twelve meters away, the person stopped and fell to her knees. Joseph raised up to get a better look.

"Joseph!" she called out, her voice cracking in pain.

Oh my God. "It's Rachel—she's been hit." His voice held disbelief.

Todd struggled with his bound hands. "Joseph, no, you can't go down there!"

Joseph was already up and running, he made it to her in seconds and pulled her up and into cover. "Rachel, are you OK? Rachel, speak to me!"

Suddenly, Joseph realized that there was something pressing against his chest. It was small and cold, and as he backed away he looked into the smiling face of Hadashah as she pointed a semi-automatic pistol at him. "You guys are so easy. Now move!"

Joseph backed toward Todd in disbelief.

"That's right Joseph it's me, and I'll finish the job that my father couldn't. I know Saul is down there without any guards. Now, where is your precious Rachel?"

Circling around to the left, Hadashah retrieved a small flashlight from her pocket and shone it along the tree line. "Rachel? Rachel! I'm not going to play any games with you. If you don't show yourself your friends are going to start dying—one by one!"

There was no response. "Rachel! Get your ass down here *now!*" Joseph could see tears of rage glistening in the corner of Hadashah's eyes.

"Don't do it Rachel!"

Hadashah's hand was a blur as the butt of her gun struck him across the face; the world spun as he hit the ground.

"I still can't believe that you all managed to get out of the plane!" Hadashah leered.

"Raaaachelll! It doesn't have to be like this you know. I know you killed my father! I was there—I was watching! Come out, and I'll spare them, even your pathetic boy-friend!"

Hadashah spun on Joseph again as the silence continued, her hands shaking. "My father's dead because of you, and my brother!" Hadashah gripped the gun with both hands. "Rachel? You better get down here. You have fifteen seconds!" As Hadashah finished talking she took a deep breath and tried to steady her hand. To their right, the sound of snapping leaves alerted them to someone's approach. Hadashah spun, a smile on her face, and shone the light.

The smile quickly faded. Keith dazedly blinked against the light, his hands still tied behind his back. Rachel burst from the brush beside them. Hadashah was quick, but she wasn't trained in hand-to-hand combat, and *krav maga* was almost a religion in the military. Rachel grabbed the weapon and turned it to the side, the barrel facing harmlessly to the side. Shoving the weapon low, Rachel torqued her grip forward. The weapon now at her own side, the pressure forced Hadashah's grip open and Rachel moved back, the pistol raised and leveled. "Move and you're dead. *J'ai pensé que vous aviez été blessé mon amour?*"

Joseph stood. "No, I am not hurt. Good work Keith."

Keith collapsed to one knee and groaned, the side of his head matted with blood.

Hadashah's eyes moved from one to the other and finally settled on Rachel. "I'd rather die than live without avenging my family." The radio squawked to life as Saul tried to contact the surface; Rachel's eyes darted to it. In her moment of distraction, Hadashah pitched her body low and to the left, out of the line of fire. A blade sprang into her hands as she closed the few feet between them.

Rachel dodged back, corrected, and fired; the solitary shot echoed into the growing dawn. Swiftly, she holstered the Glock into her waistband in the small of her back.

Hadashah's body collapsed behind her as Rachel turned back toward Joseph.

Death was instantaneous. The entire episode only lasted a few seconds.

"Damn a bear's ass!" Todd was on his feet. "You can't buy adventure like this in the states, can you Keith?" Keith managed to stand up.

Joseph helped Keith to steady and brushed the dirt from his knees. "All I've wanted since we've been in this situation is a glass of sweet iced tea."

Joseph keyed the mic, "Omega-Seven, this is Pegasus team."

"Go ahead," replied Saul.

"Ten-four, Omega-Seven, you can disregard sending any assistance. The threat has been neutralized."

"What do you mean disregard? Didn't Rachel take care of the situation?"

Joseph just stared at Rachel. "She was as efficient as usual!"

"Well, she was the only assistance that you were going to get. I'll have someone clean up the garden."

"Thank you, sir. Is there anything else?"

"No, that will be all for now. I'll call you in a couple of days and see how you're doing. Omega-Seven out!"

Joseph grabbed Rachel and pulled her close. "*Embrassez-moi madame.*"

"It would be my pleasure."

Todd leaned in and whispered, "Uh, maybe we should be getting you two to a safer location, and maybe a room."

Leaning on Todd, and rubbing his head, Keith nodded in agreement, "Where to, sir?"

"Well Keith, if Todd will turn his flashlight back on we can get out of here and back to Haifa. I believe we already have a room there."

As they all headed back up the mountain once again Todd let out an infamous "Oh Baby!" The echo resonated throughout the valley.

Standing in the doorway of the Great Hall watching the small beam of the flashlight head up the mountain, Saul could not help but think how fortunate Joseph and Rachel were to have found each other—and how blessed he was to have them as his friends. As he turned and walked back down the steps, he was lost in memory and the adventures of the childhood that they'd had in these great halls.

As he had reached the bottom step he called out, "Samuel? Where are you?"

"I am here, Your Majesty. What can I do for you?" Samuel had appeared from one of the many doorways within the great hall.

"Samuel, Sheikh Hadad's daughter is topside. I think you knew her as Hadashah. Unfortunately I believe that she chose to follow her father into death. Can you go up and make sure that she is taken care of? It's the least I can do for an old friend."

"Of course, Your Majesty. I will attend to it right away." As Samuel turned to leave, Saul's cell phone rang.

Immediately Saul looked to see the number was listed as *unknown*. Turning to make sure that Samuel had left, he flipped the phone open and answered. The voice that greeted him was one he was expecting.

"Good morning, Your Majesty. I trust that everything went according to plan?"

Saul stood erect and kept an eye on the door through which Samuel had left, "Yes. Everything is just as you had hoped."

"Wonderful. If you don't mind me asking, how many brave souls did we lose?"

"We lost Sheikh Hadad and his children. We thought we'd lost Phillip but I believe that he will be OK. He is a scrapper."

"You're right about Phillip. Please give him my regards. That's too bad about the sheikh. He was a good man."

"Thank you, sir, I will let Phillip know."

There was one last question from the caller, "Do you feel that there is anyone else that poses a threat we have not yet identified?"

Saul paused. "That would be hard to say. As long as there is something to gain I'm sure that there will always be a Judas who will want his thirty pieces of silver."

"Yes, I'm sure you are right." The caller was quiet, but he waited for an answer.

"With the sheikh and his known heirs out of the way I am certain that the secrets contained within the scrolls are secure from any further scrutiny."

"So, you have the scrolls?" There was another pause as Saul's thoughts drifted back to his two friends.

The voice on the other end prompted again, "Saul, the scrolls?"

"I apologize. I was lost in thought for a moment. The scrolls, yes—the scrolls are absolutely secure. No need to worry there."

"Very good. So, I can report to the Royal Council that the legend lives on?"

"Yes, Grand Master. Everything is just as it was. The legend lives on." Saul closed his phone and dropped it back in his pocket. He walked up the steps of the Great Hall and into the rising light of morning. Looking back up the mountain, he caught one last glimpse of the small flickering light as the helicopter traversed the hillside. A lot had happened since that cold Tuesday afternoon so many years ago.

"Take care of her, Your Majesty. Give her a kiss for me." Saul turned and walked back down the steps. He had a feeling that these would not be the last of Joseph's and Rachel's adventures. After all, life was full of chambers to explore, and who knew what truths might be found.

THE END